TAKEN

DARK LEGACY, BOOK 1

NATASHA KNIGHT

Copyright © 2018 by Natasha Knight

All rights reserved.

No part of this book may be reproduced in any form or by any electronic or mechanical means, including information storage and retrieval systems, without written permission from the author, except for the use of brief quotations in a book review.

ABOUT THIS BOOK

I'm one of four Willow daughters.
He's the first-born son of the Scafoni family. And we have history.

For generations, the Scafoni family have demanded a sacrifice of us. A virgin daughter to atone for sins so old, we don't even remember what they are anymore.

But when you have as much money as they do, you don't play by the rules. You make them.

And Sebastian Scafoni makes all the rules.

The moment I saw him, I knew he would choose me. Even though the mark on my sheath declared me unclean. Even though my beautiful sisters stood beside me, offered to him, he still chose me.

He made me his.
And then he set out to break me.

PROLOGUE

Helena

I'm the oldest of the Willow quadruplets. Four girls. Always girls. Every single quadruplet birth, generation after generation, it's always girls.

This generation's crop yielded the usual, but instead of four perfect, beautiful dolls, there were three.

And me.

And today, our twenty-first birthday, is the day of harvesting.

That's the Scafoni family's choice of words, not ours. At least not mine. My parents seem much more comfortable with it than my sisters and I do, though.

Harvesting is always on the twenty-first birthday of the quads. I don't know if it's written in stone somewhere or what, but it's what I know and what has been on the back of my mind since I learned our history five years ago.

There's an expression: *those who cannot remember the past are condemned to repeat it.* Well, that's bullshit, because we Willows know well our past and look at us now.

The same blocks that have been used for centuries standing in the old library, their surfaces softened by the feet of every other Willow Girl who stood on the same stumps of wood, and all I can think when I see them, the four lined up like they are, is how archaic this is, how fucking unreal. How they can't do this to us.

Yet, here we are.

And they are doing this to us.

But it's not *us*, really.

My shift is marked.

I'm *unclean*.

So it's really my sisters.

Sometimes I'm not sure who I hate more, my own family for allowing this insanity generation after generation, or the Scafoni monsters for demanding the sacrifice.

"It's time," my father says. His voice is grave.

He's aged these last few months. I wonder if that's remorse because it certainly isn't backbone.

I heard he and my mother argue once, exactly once, and then it was over.

He simply accepted it.

Accepted that tonight, his daughters will be made to stand on those horrible blocks while a Scafoni bastard looks us over, prods and pokes us, maybe checks our teeth like you would a horse, before making his choice. Before taking one of my sisters as his for the next three years of her life.

I'm not naive enough to be unsure what that will mean exactly. Maybe my sisters are, but not me.

"Up on the block. Now, Helena."

I look at my sisters who already stand so meekly on their appointed stumps. They're all paler than usual tonight and I swear I can hear their hearts pounding in fear of what's to come.

When I don't move right away, my father painfully takes my arm and lifts me up onto my block and all I can think, the one thing that gives me the slightest hope, is that if Sebastian Scafoni chooses me, I will find some way to end this. I won't condemn my daughters to this fate. My nieces. My granddaughters.

But he won't choose me, and I think that's why my parents are angrier than usual with me.

See, I'm the ugly duckling. At least I'd be considered ugly standing next to my sisters.

And the fact that I'm unclean—not a virgin—means I won't be taken.

The Scafoni bastard will choose one of their precious golden daughters instead.

Golden, to my dark. Golden—quite literally. Sparkling almost, my sisters.

I glance at them as my father attaches the iron shackle to my ankle. He doesn't do this to any of them. They'll do as they're told, even as their gazes bounce from the closed twelve-foot doors to me and back again and again and again.

But I have no protection to offer. Not tonight. Not on this one.

The backs of my eyes burn with tears I refuse to shed.

"How can you do this? How can you allow it?" I ask for the hundredth time. I'm talking to my mother while my father clasps the restraints on my wrists, making sure I won't attack the monsters.

"Better gag her, too."

It's my mother's response to my question and, a moment later, my father does as he's told and ensures my silence.

I hate my mother more, I think. She's a Willow quadruplet. She witnessed a harvesting herself. Witnessed the result of this cruel tradition.

Tradition.

A tradition of kidnapping.

Of breaking.

Of destroying.

I look to my sisters again. Three almost carbon

copies of each other, with long blonde hair curling around their shoulders, flowing down their backs, their blue eyes wide with fear.

Well, except in Julia's case.

She's different than the others. She's more... eager. But I don't think she has a clue what they'll do to her.

Me, no one would guess I came from the same batch.

Opposite their gold, my hair is so dark a black, it appears almost blue, with one single, wide streak of silver to relieve the stark shade, a flaw I was born with. And contrasting their cornflower-blue eyes, mine are a midnight sky; there too, the only relief the silver specks that dot them.

They look like my mother. Like perfect dolls.

I look like my great-aunt, also named Helena, down to the silver streak I refuse to dye. She's in her nineties now. I wonder if they had to lock her in her room and steal her wheelchair, so she wouldn't interfere in the ceremony.

Aunt Helena was the chosen girl of her generation. She knows what's in store for us better than anyone.

"They're coming," my mother says.

She has super hearing, I swear, but then, a moment later, I hear them too.

A door slams beyond the library, and the draft

blows out a dozen of the thousand candles that light the huge room.

A maid rushes to relight them. No electricity. Tradition, I guess.

If I were Sebastian Scafoni, I'd want to get a good look at the prize I'd be fucking for the next year. And I have no doubt there will be fucking, because what else can break a girl so completely but taking that of all things?

And it's not just the one year. No. We're given for three years. One year for each brother. Oldest to youngest. It used to be four, but now, it's three.

I would pinch my arm to be sure I'm really standing here, that I'm not dreaming, but my hands are bound behind my back, and I can't.

This can't be fucking real. It can't be legal.

And yet here we are, the four of us, naked beneath our translucent, rotting sheaths—I swear I smell the decay on them—standing on our designated blocks, teetering on them. I guess the Willows of the past had smaller feet. And I admit, as I hear their heavy, confident footfalls approaching the ancient wooden doors of the library, I am afraid.

I'm fucking terrified.

1
SEBASTIAN

Ethan and Gregory flank me as we make our way through this godforsaken house in the middle of a fucking cornfield in the middle of fucking nowhere, USA. Why in hell anyone chooses to live here is beyond me. I just hope the girl isn't a fucking dimwit. A year is a long time.

Ethan is whispering something in Gregory's ear. Gregory is even quieter than usual.

I glance back at them, and I know Greg's quiet misleads people into thinking he's the safe one, but he's not. He's the most sadistic, if you ask me. I mean, if there are degrees. Can sadism be measured in degrees?

"We decide together," Ethan says to me. He's repeated this mantra for the last forty-eight hours.

"I decide, little brother." He's twenty-five, three years my junior. Gregory is twenty-four.

"She's all of ours," he says, sounding like a fucking toddler who doesn't get his way.

"No," I clarify, and I'm trying to be patient because really, I can't blame Ethan for being the way he is. "She's mine."

"She's only yours first."

"Give it a rest, Ethan," I say.

"Sebastian." My stepmother's heels click over the hardwood. "Don't fight with your brother. You know I don't like to see that." She goes to Ethan, touches his cheek. "You'll all have your turn with the Willow whore. They're resilient."

Her loathing of the Willow women is so obvious, a part of me wishes the chosen girl luck because she'll need it to walk out of the Scafoni home when her three years are up. It'll take someone with a spine of steel to survive my stepmother, never mind my brothers and me.

"Why do you hate them, Lucinda?" I ask, enjoying my power over her.

Truth be told, she probably hates me as much as the Willows, but it doesn't matter. I may not be her biological son, but I am master of the Scafoni family. My father is dead, I am the eldest, and I have no intention of letting anyone rule me or usurp my place, especially not Lucinda.

"They're whores, Sebastian. There to serve a purpose. Remember that instead of turning on your brothers. Family first. Never forget it."

"You don't have to remind me of that, Lucinda. I just wish I understood your hatred of them. I mean, what are they to you? You're not a Scafoni by blood, after all."

This irritates the fuck out of her, and that fact makes me grin.

The library doors open, saving her from having to answer.

A thousand candles burn inside, casting a warm glow over the large room. I'm not sure which scent is stronger, that of old books, of melting wax or fear.

I spy the first white sheath, and as much as I like to tell myself this is nothing more than a family obligation, a thrill runs through me.

I'm excited to claim my Willow Girl.

Lucinda falls back, as is her place.

I step forward and turn to my right, where Mr. and Mrs. Willow, the proud parents of this generation's crop, stand with ghostly faces. I nod my greeting. I am civil, at least.

I take in the room, still avoiding the girls on their blocks, saving them for last, appreciating the ancient library—the only thing old about this house, the rest having been rebuilt ten years ago, and it was done cheaply too. I hate cheap. But I guess by then, the money from the previous reaping was running out.

Based on old sketches, this house was once a grand estate, before the fire that ravaged it years ago. But the library is the most important room, the one kept up to par, as per the contract. And it's the only one I care about.

Beautiful old wooden beams overhead keep the roof from collapsing on our heads, and arched windows reflect the scene within. I wonder how bright it is during the day. If you can see particles of dust a thousand years old disturbed when ghosts rummage through the old tomes, searching for a way out of this nightmare for their girls.

I harden at the thought, and for a moment, I understand Lucinda's hatred. The Willows aren't the only ones cursed to repeat this ancient, insane tradition.

A candle flickers.

I wonder if the dead Willow Girls of generations past stand witness to tonight's harvesting.

It's with this thought in mind that I let my gaze come to rest on the spectacle before me.

Four girls.

Four beauties, because the Willow's only breed beauties.

Three dolls, perfect with their golden hair and enormous blue eyes. One...well...I cock my head to the side at the sight of her. This one is bound, her arms stretched behind her. A gag covers her mouth.

And on the belly of her shift, there's a streak of red.

Pig's blood.

I decide to save her for last.

I move to the first, let my gaze slide over her. She drops hers to the floor, where it should have been all along. I sweep her from head to toe and back. The sheath doesn't offer much cover, but that's the point. They are to be laid out for my perusal. For me to take my pick.

Because I am fortunate enough to be born a Scafoni and they unfortunate enough to be born a Willow.

This one is pretty enough. Perfect, actually. But I move on to her sister.

Another doll-like girl.

She doesn't drop her gaze to her feet but keeps it just beyond me. It's high time the Willows were reminded of their place.

This one has something different in her eyes. She's coquettish, almost. And she's making eyes at my brother. From the look of her, I'm surprised she's not the one with the blood marking on her sheath.

With her, I'll be bored. And she won't survive a single month, much less three years.

Sadly, there are no trade-ins. Once the choice is made, it is made, and if the girl dies before her time is completed, well, our loss, I guess.

It's unfair, really.

I step to my left, to the next block, the next girl.

Just like her sisters.

I'm too anxious to reach the last one to spend any time on this one because perfection like this, it doesn't interest me. I need more than physical beauty.

Where is the fun in breaking a girl when she doesn't have a spine to break? Where is the game in walking a meek little lamb to the slaughter?

I'd prefer a cat, wild and feral, with sharp teeth and a sharper tongue.

With this thought in mind, I step to the last Willow Girl.

She isn't a doll. Not like her sisters, at least. Beautiful, still, but this one, there's something about her, a darkness to her. Rebellion burning inside her.

Or maybe it's just arrogance.

It makes one corner of my mouth curve upward.

This one is no lamb. I see it in the icy midnight eyes that greet me, and I realize why she's bound and gagged. She'd lunge at me if she could, and the thought makes my dick hard.

I walk a circle around her and confirm that her wrists are bound in leather restraints at her lower back. Not only that, but she's shackled to the block. I guess they weren't taking any chances.

When I face her again, she doesn't shy away, this girl, but holds my gaze. And right now, I want nothing more than to punish her for it.

She's different than the others. I decide to call them the dolls. This one, her dark hair is so black it's almost blue. It falls straight and heavy down her back, long enough to wind around my hand, thick enough to withstand my fist.

I step to her, and even standing on the block, she has to turn her head up to keep my gaze, but she does.

"Switch on the lights," I command.

I want to see the bounty. Fuck tradition.

The room is drenched in bright light on my order, and Ethan is quick to step toward me.

"Not her. Take any other one but her." It's irritating, the sound of his voice. Like a fucking fly that keeps buzzing at my ear.

I don't acknowledge him or his comment. He needs to learn his place sometime.

My eyes are locked on the girl. She stands watching, defiant.

Petite, almost. Maybe 5'4" off the block, I'd guess. A good foot shorter than me. She's naked beneath the sheath, as instructed. I look down at the dark pink points of her nipples, cold beneath my inspection, pressing against the centuries-old cloth.

I study her, keep her gaze as I gather the sheath in my hand and stretch it, holding the marked spot out.

"I'm sorry," her mother says.

I turn to the woman. She lowers her gaze, and her husband steps forward, then bows his head in apology.

Because what that streak of blood means is that she failed the examination. This one isn't a virgin.

I fist the cloth and bare her feet, her knees, thighs, pussy. That's when I look down, when I feel that thick mound of dark curls at my fingers.

She stiffens, exhales audibly, and if I listen hard, I think I can hear her scream on the inside.

"Lower your gaze," I tell her, squeezing the hair, making her wince.

She lifts her chin higher, and I see the workings of her throat as she swallows.

"Do as he says!"

It's her father. And I want to kill him for his intrusion. She's mine. I will be the one to teach her. I will be the one to punish her.

"Lower. Your. Gaze."

I curl my fingers down to cup her pussy.

She falters, and for the first time, I see the terror in her eyes. It overtakes the hate. She blinks, her spine bends, and finally, she drops her gaze to her naked feet.

I release her, step back, and watch the sheath drop to cover her. I feel her on my fingers, and I don't wipe the damp away.

"Her name?"

"Helena, sir."

It must burn to call a man half your age sir.

"Helena." I try it out. I think I'll keep it. "What's this?" I pick up the silver streak of hair.

"It grows that way. She's had it since she was a small child. It's in my wife's family."

Yes, it is. I remember now.

And I know she's the one I have to take. Perfectly imperfect. Opposite her sisters.

Flawed.

Her hair feels like silk in my hand. Heavy, smooth silk.

I nod, turn my back.

"Her," I say and walk out of the room.

2

HELENA

I'm given one hour to say good-bye.

I pack no clothes. I take nothing personal. I'm not allowed, not even a single photograph, not my books, nothing.

This is harder than I thought. Maybe I'm not as strong as I thought.

Sebastian Scafoni chose me.

I am to be the next Willow Girl.

There was no way I should have been picked—not with my sisters among the pickings, not with the blood marking my sheath—and I am unprepared.

I'm wearing a black dress. It's my funeral dress. Yes, at twenty-one, I own a designated funeral dress. It's an A-line that covers me from just below my knees right up to my neck. Lace creates a complicated pattern along my collarbones and down my arms that's only relieved in a ruffle at my throat and wrists.

It's pretty, but I didn't choose it to look pretty. I chose it because this occasion, it's like a funeral and I want them all—Willow and Scafoni alike—to know I am in mourning.

Along with the dress, I put on my favorite Dr. Martens. I've had them forever and they look like it, but like I said, I'm not going for pretty.

Inside the Dr. Martens I've slipped my pocketknife, and to finish off my look, my hair's in a tight ponytail and I'm wearing no makeup.

And for as defiant as I may appear, I'm sitting on the edge of my bed and hugging my pillow to myself and trying not to cry.

Crap.

What a fool I am, thinking myself stronger than my sisters. Better able to survive this.

What he did in the library, how he…handled me, for lack of a better word—it makes me burn with humiliation. But also something else. Something that makes no sense. And if he can make me feel so confused in a matter of moments, what will he do in years?

What will be left of me when this is finished?

I shove the thought from my mind.

I can't dwell there. I won't.

As much as I try not to, my mind wanders to the

last Willow Girl. She was my mother's older sister. I was five when she came home, and I remember how she looked when she did. I remember how afraid of her I'd been because I'd thought her a ghost.

And she became one, soon enough. I still remember how she smelled when I went up to the attic that late summer night.

My bedroom door opens, and I quickly wipe the tears off my face and stand, dropping the pillow back on the bed and turning to see my mother wheeling my Great-aunt Helena into my room.

It takes all I have not to break down when I see her. Because if I'm to be gone for three years, I know I won't ever see her again.

"Close the door," Aunt Helena instructs my mother sharply.

"Aunty—" my mother starts.

My aunt doesn't take her eyes off me. Even at her age, they're fierce. And I've never been able to figure out why she's never liked my mother.

"Leave us alone," she says.

Without another word, my mother closes the door.

I go to her, wheel her forward. She has an old-fashioned chair and it's unwieldy, but she refuses a new one, one more comfortable.

Once I have her closer to the edge of the bed, I sit and face her. She reaches out her hands, and I set mine in hers. The contrast in youth and age is striking, hers like parchment, the bone delicate. Mine youthful. Full of life.

"I knew he would choose you," she says.

And this time, I do cry. I wipe the back of one hand across my face.

She watches me, and she's so strong. She doesn't shed a single tear. I've never seen her cry, in fact. Not once.

"There's a reason it was you, child."

She squeezes my hands and makes me look at her. Her hair, although it's thinned out, is still as black as mine, that silver streak as bright. She's grown smaller, though. I guess I have to remember I'm lucky to have had her this long. She's almost a century old.

"I'm scared," I say, lowering my gaze when I do, ashamed of my fear when she is so strong.

She squeezes my hands, and I look up again.

"I was scared when it was me."

"You're the strongest woman I know."

"Not then. Not at first. I was afraid just like you are. But our ancestors watched over me, and they are watching over you now. They chose you, Helena. The Willow ancestors chose you."

She lets go of my hands, and I watch how hers tremble as she reaches into the high neck of her dress to pull out a chain I've not seen before. She always wears turtleneck sweaters or dresses, always has her neck covered, even in summer. She holds the thing in the palm of her hand and studies it. I wish I could see her eyes, know what she's thinking.

But when she snaps the chain with a quick strength I didn't know she still had, I gasp in surprise. She lets it slide through her fingers and onto the floor and looks at me, opening her palm.

I look down at the ring there, the strangest ring I've ever seen.

The band itself is a yellow white, and there are three stones on it. Three jagged amethysts so dark, they're a purple-black. She turns the ring, and I lean in closer because there's a small skull carved into one side of it.

"It's made of bone," she says, her eyes wide when I look at her.

"Bone?" I'm a little creeped out, honestly.

"Know that not every Willow Girl is broken by them. I wasn't. I took from them as they took from me and I survived."

She takes the ring and slides it onto my middle finger. It's a perfect fit. She then closes her hand over it, squeezes and brings her face closer to mine.

"It's up to you, Helena. Destroy their line and end this. It's why you were chosen. It's time to finish with this insanity."

My mouth falls open.

Before I can even fully process what she has said,

the door opens. It's my father and behind him, my sisters, all in their jeans and T-shirts, hair in braids, looking like it's a normal day. Like what just took place in the library didn't happen at all. Like I'm not wearing my funeral dress waiting to be taken.

"The car is here."

I draw back and look at my aunt again. I wonder at the faith she's putting in me, because she's wrong. I'm not that strong.

She nods once, and I hug her, and she holds me so tight that she presses tears from my eyes.

"You have to hate them to survive them, child. To destroy them," she whispers before pulling back. "Remember to hate them."

I stand and take one last look at her, straighten my spine, and walk out the door, out of my house, and into the keeping of my enemy.

I'M DRIVEN IN A LUXURY SUV BY A DRIVER WITH A face as stony as those carved into Mt. Rushmore two hours to a small, private airfield I didn't know existed.

It's dark when we arrive, although not as dark as the Willow property. No light pollution there. Here, the lights of the airport, even though it's small, spoil the night sky.

It's easier now that I'm out of the house. Easier

not to have to look at my sisters' faces, my parents' faces.

But as the car slows to turn through the gradually opening gates and I see the other SUVs there, the gathering of people in the headlights, the waiting jet, my trepidation grows.

I am alone.

With my thumb I touch my aunt's ring and think about what she said. I try to imagine her younger, my age, and in the same position, and I can. Except that she's a much stronger version of me. A fiercer one.

The driver slows to a stop, and the heads of two men and one woman turn to watch.

It's the brothers, Ethan and Gregory. I know their names.

They're in the same suits they wore to the ceremony. Sebastian is talking with the pilot. He hasn't bothered to look in my direction. I guess he has all the time in the world.

Ethan is already grinning like a hyena. Do hyena's grin? I guess I picture him as that sort of animal. A scavenger.

"There's a reason it was you, child."

Maybe my aunt is right. Maybe it's best I'm the Willow Girl.

But I can't help the feeling that I'm somehow expendable. Like if I don't survive, my family will.

They'll go on without me, and when the next generation comes of age, the library will again be lit with a thousand candles as one of my sisters puts her daughters on their designated blocks, thanking her lucky stars she wasn't the Willow Girl.

Will I even be there to witness it?

I know I'm different than my sisters, pretty much in every way. The outside is just a reflection of everything inside. I'm the one they look up to, the one they used to come to when they had a bad dream, the one who has always protected them.

But right now, I don't feel very strong.

Lucinda Scafoni is wearing a pair of wide-legged, high-waisted black pants with a cream-colored blouse. Her dark hair is pinned into a bun, and it's so tight that it distorts her face a little. Her eyes are narrow, calculated slits as she watches me, unblinking.

I wonder if she can see through the tinted windows because she's looking right at me.

Gregory, the youngest Scafoni, is as handsome as Sebastian. I'd know they were brothers just from the resemblance in features.

Not Ethan, though. Ethan looks very different.

Gregory simply stands looking on, almost bored, giving away nothing of what he's thinking, and something tells me to be careful with him. He's not as uninterested as he appears.

The driver opens my door and doesn't quite meet my eyes. He's Italian too, I can tell. They all have that olive skin and dark hair that belongs to the Mediterranean-born. I wonder if he even speaks English because he doesn't look like an American-Italian.

But what do I know about American-Italians? I was born and grew up in the Midwest. I've traveled some with my family, but those occasions were rare. My parents usually went places alone and left us safely tucked away on the property.

I guess I understand why now.

It's when I step out of the SUV and the driver shuts the door that Sebastian finishes with the pilot and finally deigns to look my way. His gaze sweeps my dress, hovers at my choice of footwear, then meets my eyes.

One side of his mouth curves upward.

I've already seen that look, and I hate it. It's his victory smirk. His *I scare you and I know it* triumph.

I steel my spine and straighten. In that instant, I decide I can do it. That I must do it. It's him or me. Survival of the fittest.

And I have to be the fittest.

From my periphery, I see that his mother—bored, I guess—turns and heads up the jet stairs, giving the order to "Bring her," as she disappears into the plane.

The driver takes hold of my arm when I don't move.

The three brothers stand watching me, and it takes all I have to keep my eyes locked on Sebastian's as I'm made to close the distance between us.

I'm an idiot because I feel that pang of attraction, like I did when I first saw him, even through the hate.

"Where are you taking me?" I ask when I stand before him.

I didn't think about this part, didn't think I'd be a plane ride away from my family.

"You don't speak unless spoken to, Willow Girl," Ethan says, cocking his head to the side as if daring me to challenge him.

I raise my head and narrow my eyes. My hands fist at my sides. He takes a step toward me.

"I wasn't speaking to you," I say.

Gregory chuckles, but my heart races as Ethan's face reddens.

I'm grateful that before I have to back away, Sebastian's hand closes over his shoulder. All I can do is look at it and think how big it is.

"Get on the plane, Ethan."

"She needs to learn—"

"I'll take care of it. Go on."

Ethan's black eyes haven't left mine during this exchange. I force my lips into a smirk.

He shoves Sebastian's hand off and leans his face into mine.

"Smile now, whore. You won't be when it's my turn to have you."

Being called a whore by him doesn't bother me, for some reason, but his threat—I know he'll make good on it. If he even waits his turn.

He spins on his heel and doesn't give me another glance as he, too, disappears into the belly of the plane.

When he's gone, I swallow and look at Gregory, who is watching me with silent interest, and all I can think is I'll be his too.

What state will I be in by the time it's his turn to have me?

Gregory turns and boards the plane, so it's just me and Sebastian.

"My brother is right. You speak when spoken to. Get on the plane."

"What's wrong with him?"

"You should be more respectful."

"Where are you taking me?"

He exhales loudly, like he was expecting that, expecting me to be disobedient.

When he reaches out for me, I take a step back, but that big hand closes around my arm, and I'm trapped.

He smiles. "I knew you'd be like this," he says, turning me, marching me to the stairs and up them and it's like I'm ascending the scaffold to my execution.

A few minutes later, we're seated inside the luxury jet and taking off into the night sky to a destination I do not yet know, to the beginning of a life I'm less and less sure I will survive.

3

SEBASTIAN

I'm watching her from my place at the table where Lucinda has insisted we play a card game to pass the time. The flight to Venice will take all night and part of the morning.

The girl has finally fallen asleep. For the first two hours, she kept her eyes locked on the window like she could chart the night sky, guess her destination.

Not that where we're going is a secret. I just like fucking with her more than I thought I would.

I didn't want this at first. I didn't like the whole idea of it, the tradition of essentially kidnapping a girl. But it is our tradition, and as the eldest, the duty falls on me.

And now, well, I look forward to having this pretty, willful Willow Girl to do with as I please. Because when all is said and done, I am a man.

And any man who says he doesn't want a girl on her knees at his feet is a liar.

"Your turn, Sebastian," Lucinda says.

She too gives the girl a sideways glance, but she's more interested in *my* reactions to Helena. She'll take her opportunities with the girl. I wonder which of us Helena will hate more.

"Hard to focus with a hard-on, huh, brother?" Ethan asks. "Why not wake her up? Initiate her in the bedroom? I would. I mean, she's used goods anyway. You should have taken one of the others."

I don't react to his taunt. I've lived with his jealousy for more than twenty years of my life. From the moment he was born. Instead, I lay down my cards, winning this hand of Pinochle, a favorite game of Lucinda's.

"There. How's that?"

I stand and swallow the last of my whiskey before handing it to one of the two attendants for a refill.

When I take the seat beside Helena, she stirs, blinks her eyes open, and looks around her, startled.

I know the moment she remembers where she is. I see her throat work when she swallows and sits up in her seat.

The attendant hands me my drink, and I take a sip.

"I need to use the bathroom," she says, not quite looking at me.

I rise to my feet.

It takes her a minute to unbuckle the seat belt, but she does the same.

I gesture for her to walk ahead of me to the door at the back, the greedy eyes of my family following us.

When we reach the door, I lean around her to open it, and she stops for a minute. I guess she's not expecting a bedroom. Her face goes white as a ghost's, and there's only panic in her eyes when she turns to me.

"Bathroom's in there."

She doesn't trust me, and she shouldn't, but she walks into the room. I close the door behind us.

"There," I say, pointing to the bathroom door.

She disappears behind it, and I sit down in the armchair to wait. I cross one leg over the other and check the time. We still have four hours to go, and I'm bored.

I set my drink down and roll up my shirt sleeves, listen to the toilet flush, hear the water at the sink go on, then off.

She doesn't emerge right away, though, and I imagine her in there, giving herself a pep talk.

Ten minutes pass before the door opens, and she steps into the bedroom. She looks around. She takes in literally every detail of the room so as to avoid having to look at me.

I'm a patient man. I wait until she has no choice but to meet my gaze.

"Why did you bring me in here?"

"I thought you'd be more comfortable on the bed. You were asleep—"

"I wasn't asleep." She glances at the bed. She doesn't believe me that it's concern for her comfort, and she's right not to.

Any normal person would feel pity for her, but not me. I like her fear. It gets my heart pumping, blood flowing. Gets my dick hard.

"Is it starting already?" she asks, her voice breaking a little.

"Is what starting already?" I ask, as if I don't understand.

She shakes her head, opens her mouth, then closes it again, points to the bed. "I mean, what you want from me, we both know what that is."

"What do I want from you?"

She looks at me, narrows her eyes. "I'm not going to play your stupid games."

I uncross my legs, smiling as I rise, go to her.

She stands her ground, even when I get into her space, but flinches when I raise my hand to her face, almost touching her cheek, but not.

Instead, I set her hair behind her shoulders and take a moment to feel the texture of it, feel the difference of the black strands as opposed to the silver streak.

I lean in close to her, inhale her scent. She's trembling a little.

"That's too bad, because I like games," I say.

I step back, look her over, then return to my seat, pick up my drink, and take a sip. I cross my leg over my knee again. "Your shoes are hideous."

She looks down at them, gives me a little smirk when she looks back at me. "I like them."

"Drink?" I ask her while I sip mine.

She shakes her head no.

"Sit down."

"I'm fine."

"Are you going to stand for four more hours?"

She looks beyond me out the window, but it's still night. "Where are we going?"

"Venice."

"Venice? As in Italy?"

"Yes."

"But...you can't..." She sits on the edge of the bed, almost falls into it, and tugs the sleeves of the pretty black dress down into her palms.

I notice the strange ring on her finger.

She turns back to me with something like hope in her eyes. "I don't have a passport."

I almost chuckle. "I'll stop the captain immediately, then. Tell him to turn the plane around. Call the whole thing off." I extinguish that hope like a candle and I know it's cruel to do it but it's too easy and I can't resist. And really, like a passport would matter if it was even true. "I have your passport. Your mother knew the rules. Everything was arranged, as it should be."

"You're a jerk."

I shrug a shoulder.

She puts her fists to her forehead and squeezes her eyes shut. "I don't understand."

"We're going to the Scafoni estate in Venice. There's not much to understand. You will be comfortable—"

"Comfortable?" She snaps her gaze to me. "I will be anything but comfortable. Your brothers look at me like I'm a piece of meat. Your mother looks like she wants to stab me. And you...you..."

I'm on my feet and so is she. "No one's going to stab you, Helena. Don't be dramatic."

She stops, looks up at me. "Don't be dramatic?"

I don't comment. I know it'll take her time to accept her situation.

"Is this funny to you? Putting me and my sisters up on blocks like we're slaves to be auctioned off, dressing us in decaying old...parchment—"

"It was hardly parchment—"

"Looking us over, one by one, judging us while your brothers look on, one of whom could barely keep his dick in his pants while you...you—"

"Settle down," I warn, and when I step toward her, she backs up.

"While you touched me like you did. You're

sick, all of you, but especially you! You think this is funny? Kidnapping is funny? Making someone a slave to you, to your family, is funny?"

"Not just someone," I say, closing the space between us so her back is to the wall. "You."

She raises her arm to slap me, but I catch her wrist. "Don't ever do that."

She tries with her other arm, and I capture that one too. I raise both of them over her head and lean into her, pressing her back to the wall.

"Do you have a hearing problem, Willow Girl?"

"My name is Helena."

"Your name is Willow Girl when I want it to be Willow Girl."

She tries to free her arms, but she's trapped. When she tries to knee me, I capture her leg between my thighs. And then she does something totally unexpected.

She spits.

Right in my face.

Instinctively, I transfer both of her wrists into one of my hands and raise my arm, palm flat, ready to strike, but she lets out a half-scream, and I stop because what the fuck am I doing?

Her eyes are huge, and I wonder if she isn't as shocked with what she just did as I am.

I lower my hand, the one that was ready to slap her, and wipe off the spit, rage building inside me like lava coming up a volcano on the edge of erupting.

I grip her jaw and force her face up, look at her features, pretty and delicate. She's so much smaller than me. My hand next to her face, it's huge.

"Be careful, Willow Girl. I can crush you."

When she blinks, tears streak down her cheeks.

I watch her; wild horses couldn't drag my attention from her right now. I am lost in her sad, frightened, midnight-colored eyes. The blue is lighter when she cries and she's so fucking pretty right now, so soft and vulnerable and afraid with her wet face, her swollen lips and wide eyes.

Some women are prettiest when they cry. She's one of them. And I want her tears. It's sick, I know. A disease. I'm sick. But I want them.

"Won't you crush me anyway?" she asks, her voice barely a whisper. "But is that all you'll do? All your brothers will do?"

I release her and step back. I understand her meaning. We don't take the Willow Girl for her conversation skills. She'll be our toy in every way. And this part, I can't kick the fact that it bothers me.

"You stay in here and try to wrap your brain around your situation."

"Stay in here? Where would I go? We're on a fucking airplane."

"Take this time to come to fucking terms with the fact that I own you."

"Fuck you."

I snort. "Want some advice, Helena?" I ask, taking her by the arms. Squeezing. "Try to figure out how not to piss me off. It might help you to remember that *you belong to me*. That I am your master, and that I will be obeyed. Are we clear?"

When she doesn't answer right away, I give her a shake.

"Are we?" I ask.

"Yes!"

"Good" I go to the door,

"I saw Libby," she whispers. "She was my aunt."

I stop, my hand on the doorknob.

"The last Willow Girl," she says, as if I need that clarified.

I straighten. I know.

I remember Libby.

I turn to her. "Have a fucking drink. Have ten. Get yourself together."

Her chest heaves with a sob, and she wipes the back of her hand across her face.

I open the door and walk out into the main room where my family, my fucking family, has been enjoying the entertainment.

"She givin' you some trouble, brother?" Ethan asks, picking the olive out of his drink and tossing it into his mouth. "Told you that you should have taken one of the others. They were prettier anyway. Mama, don't you think so? They were prettier."

Lucinda ignores him. "You should whip her, Sebastian. The instant we arrive. It's the only thing that works on the Willow whores."

She drains her martini.

I go to the liquor cart, yank the glass out of the attendant's hand, and pour myself a double. I take a long sip before turning to them.

"I'm glad you enjoyed the show, but where it concerns *my* Willow Girl, mind your own fucking business."

4

HELENA

I do as he says, but only after sitting on the bed for a while and feeling sorry for myself.

I'm wasting tears on them, on my enemy. I'm weak. God, not twenty-four hours ago, I was staring him down, ready for him, wanting him to choose me only because I thought he wouldn't.

But I'm pathetic and weak.

I get up off the bed and pick up the glass he left unfinished and drain it. I don't especially like whiskey, but I force it down and pour more. Pour another, generous glass of the stuff. It's inelegant, I know, but I don't care.

I sit on the edge of the bed and drink it like it's water, and when I'm finished with it, I crawl onto the bed with my hideous shoes still on my feet and lay down on my side and I cry some more.

He's right. I need to get myself together. But first, I need to get this out of my system. Get my fear gone.

I look at my aunt's ring. She thinks I'm strong, but she's wrong. I'm weak. So weak. So opposite her.

When my mother sat us down on our sixteenth birthday and told us this part of Willow history, I swore I wouldn't be the Willow Girl because it scared the fuck out of me. And as soon as I could, I made sure I wouldn't pass the virginity requirement, thinking it would save me.

So yeah, I'm weak.

A coward.

"There's a reason it was you, child."

I sit up, reach into my boot, and take out pocketknife. I've had it forever, but never even dissected a worm with it. I open it now, touch the sharp point, press it into the tip of my finger until I draw a drop of blood.

"They chose you, Helena. The Willow ancestors chose you."

I wish I knew more about our history. I wish I'd studied the books in the library rather than pretending it wasn't real. That it was an archaic tradition. That I was safe.

I don't know what binds the Willows and the Scafonis. What has bound us for generations. When I was little, and my Aunt Libby returned home, we were told she'd been on a trip. I was too young to ask questions. That same summer, she slit her wrists on the old bed in the attic of the Willow family home.

I think the only reason my parents didn't make up some story was because I'm the one who found her.

I remember I used to be afraid of the attic. Always thought there were ghosts there. My room was just below it, and the only reason I went up there at all was because the blood had finally dripped through a crack in my ceiling and onto my foot.

Drip, drip, drip.

The window was open. It was the hottest summer I remember. The air-conditioning didn't work as well on the third floor, and it was hard to sleep in the heat.

When I woke up, I saw the drops of red on my foot. I remember thinking how strange it looked and wondering what it was when another drop fell, and I looked up to see the stain on the ceiling.

Every time I remember that night, I can't for the life of me figure out why I went up there. Why I didn't go wake my parents. But I didn't. I took my flashlight and my teddy bear, and I climbed the creaky old stairs to the attic.

I remember when I first saw my aunt lying in that bed. I went over to her to ask her why she wasn't sleeping in her room where it wasn't so hot. That's when I saw the pool of drying blood she was lying in. Saw how unnatural her color was, how gray.

She used to be so pretty whenever I looked at photographs of my mother and her sisters. Aunt Libby was the prettiest of them all in fact.

But not after she came back home from her years with the Scafoni family. They stole her beauty. Her youth. And ultimately, her life.

I turn the ring on my finger, look at the skull, the hollowed-out eyes, smear the droplet of blood over the bone.

It's made of bone. How does someone do that? I turn it again and feel the three sharp tips of the amethysts.

"They chose you, Helena."

I lay back down and close my eyes. I'm tired. I don't think he'll come back in here. I don't think he'll allow his brothers or mother in either. I do know without a doubt that Sebastian Scafoni is in charge of his family. Even his mother.

I just don't know what that means for me.

———

WHEN I WAKE UP, I AM AGAIN DISORIENTED.

We're no longer flying. I can tell before I even blink my eyes open because I no longer hear the constant, dull noise of the plane in the air. My mouth feels like cotton. I'm thirsty. Did we land?

I open my eyes and am startled to find myself in a large bed in a huge bedroom. The walls are a creamy white, and there are two windows against one of them. Heavy drapes the color of old paper are pulled closed, but the sun is trying to creep in from the split between the panels.

There is a large dresser that looks like an antique against the far wall and a sitting area with a lilac chaise. A small, round side table with three delicate legs stands beside it and another, larger one stands on the other side.

I sit up a little. The satin blanket falls away, and I realize I'm naked.

A peek tells me I'm completely naked.

Someone must have undressed me. Was the whiskey so strong that I don't remember landing and don't remember being stripped of my clothes after being carried into this room?

A momentary sensory inventory tells me I haven't been violated—apart from this stripping of my clothes.

I pull the cover back up to my chin and swing my legs over the side of the bed. I switch on the lamp on the nightstand because apart from that strip of sunlight at the windows, it's dark inside. The lamp is pretty, one of those Tiffany Venetian ones with a variety of colors of glass. The only other item on the nightstand is my pocketknife.

Whoever undressed me let me keep it?

I get up and tug the blanket off the bed, wrap it around myself.

There's another door that I can see leads to a bathroom, so I go to it, creeping slowly, although I can't imagine anyone's hiding in there. And I was definitely sleeping alone.

Once I'm in the bathroom, I close the door and switch on the light. It's big, big enough for a tub for two at one end, a separate stand-up shower, also for two, a walled-off toilet, and two pedestal sinks.

There's a large window above the bathtub. It's stained glass, and the sun casts a pretty purplish-blue light into the room. I discover it's sealed, so it can't be opened, and I can't look outside to try to figure out where I am. Try to figure out how hard it will be to run away and disappear.

Although I can't do that.

The tile along the floors and ceilings is a creamy white, and the fixtures are brushed nickel. A rack along one wall holds a dozen plush towels as well as a variety of shampoos, conditioners, body washes, oils, and anything else a woman may need.

And it is for a woman. Prepared in advance for the Willow Girl. I can tell from the smell of a few of the luxury products.

Wishing there was a lock on the door, I quickly use the toilet, then go to one of the sinks to wash my hands and face.

There's a brand-new toothbrush and a tube of

toothpaste beside it. I unwrap the former, smear it with toothpaste, and brush my teeth as I take in my reflection, my bed-head hair, the shadows under my eyes. The fingerprints he left behind in the form of bruises along my jaw.

When I'm done brushing my teeth, I locate the wooden hairbrush I'd seen and work it through my hair, smoothing out the bed-head look. I set it down and open the bedroom door and stop dead in my tracks because the curtains have been pulled back to let in the bright sunlight and Sebastian is on the bed, in the space I just vacated, wearing jeans and a black T-shirt, looking much more casual than he had last night in his suit.

Both of his arms are tattooed, which surprises me for some reason, and he's leaning against the headboard and reading something on his phone, but when he sees me, he tucks the phone into his pocket.

"Where's my dress?" I ask.

He looks me over with the blanket wrapped awkwardly around me and smiles. He seems refreshed, like he got some sleep and had a shower.

"I took it off when I brought you in. I thought you'd be more comfortable naked."

"You thought wrong. I'm not."

"Did you take me literally when I said to have ten drinks?"

"No. I just had one. Maybe two. Was it drugged?

Is that why I didn't wake up when we landed? Are you going to keep me drugged too?"

He chuckles, swings his legs off the bed, and stands. "Relax, sweetheart."

"I'm not your sweetheart. Where are my clothes?"

He picks up the pocketknife. "This? Really? Hidden in your boot?"

I walk to him and go to grab it out of his hand, but he pulls it away and grips my wrist with his other hand.

"It's mine," I say, twisting to pull free.

He's too strong, though. I won't be free until he decides to let me go.

"And now it's mine."

He pockets it and releases me.

I stumble backward.

He comes toward me, and I take a step away, but my back is to the wall. He closes his hands around my arms, rubs them once.

"I'm not fucking stupid, Helena. You'll only hurt yourself trying to injure me."

"I want my clothes," I say, knowing he's right.

"I like you like this," he says, letting his eyes fall to my chest where the satin is wrapped so uselessly around me.

"Did you touch me too?"

"Not yet," he says. "I don't get off on bedding women who are passed out drunk."

"You're good with kidnapping though?"

"I guess."

He's so fucking cocky, I want to smash his beautiful face in.

"Do you prefer us to fight? Is that it? I mean, what you do, you and your family? What's the difference if the woman, *the Willow Girl*, is passed out or not? Maybe it's easier on her if she is. I mean, let's be honest here. I don't imagine it's your moral sense of—"

But I never get a chance to finish whatever the hell it was I was starting because he shoots one of his arms out and wraps his hand around my throat and he squeezes.

"Be careful," he warns, leaning in close to my face, inhaling my scent as if he can smell my fear. He brings his lips to my cheek, and a moment later, I feel the scruff of his jaw along the shell of my ear. "Be very careful, Willow Girl."

I shudder. His words are like physical things, three-dimensional and powerful.

He's squeezing so hard that he's lifting me on tiptoe, and I realize I've let go of the blanket and it's slid to pool around my feet. I have both hands wrapped around his thick forearm, clawing at him, digging tracks into his skin, trying to drag him off me.

"Had enough?"

A garbled sound comes from my throat and one

of my arms falls to my side. It's only then that he releases me. I slide to the floor, gasping for breath, my neck tender.

He steps back. "Maybe Lucinda's right," he says, and I wonder why he calls his mother by her first name, but I don't have time to think about it. "I should take you out to the post. Whip you now, get it over with. Is that how you want it?"

I look up at him. Is he serious?

Yes. He is. And he would. I mean, this whole situation, it's archaic. Like we've gone back in time a hundred years. A thousand.

"Is it, Willow Girl?"

"Don't call me that."

"You don't like sweetheart. You don't like Willow Girl. Tell me, do you need me to whip you?" he asks, nudging my hip with the toe of his shoe.

I shake my head, hug my knees to myself, and look straight ahead. Anywhere but at his mocking eyes.

"Get up."

I shake my head again. I can see the goose bumps that have risen on my arms, making the faint dusting of hair stand on end.

"Get up, Helena. Don't make me make you."

I grab hold of the fallen blanket, but he steps on it. When I look up at him, his dark eyes are narrowed and intense.

"No blanket. I want to see you."

Hasn't he seen enough? I want to ask him, but I don't. I can't push him too far.

"I'm tired of repeating myself with you," he says.

I rise slowly to my feet, covering myself as best I can with my arms, keeping my legs close together, letting my hair fall to shield me like I'm Lady Godiva on her horse.

He steps back a little, and the silence between us is heavy, like it can be put on a scale and weighed.

It feels like it's sitting on my lungs, that weight, suffocating me.

"Look at me."

It takes me a long minute to do so, to meet his slate eyes, and when I do, it's like I'm in another dimension, another world.

It's just him and me and this silence.

It's too much. Too loud.

Deafening.

And as I study him, there's something that won't let me look away.

If I'd met him under different circumstances, I'd find him attractive, not scary, but it's not that which has me caught like an animal in a trap.

He's the hunter and I'm the prey.

He and I, we're connected somehow, and maybe it's our shared history or our bound destiny, this insane game we have to play out.

I don't know what it is, but it is. It's there.

The ring on my finger weighs heavy.

Bone.

I suddenly know what my aunt meant.

The ring, it's made of human bone. I know it.

I imagine my aunt in this room. I wonder if it looked the same then. If I'm sleeping on the bed she once slept on. I imagine her standing here, much as I am now, facing off with her Scafoni master, because that is what they are. What Sebastian is. My master.

The word boils inside my gut, and I fist my hands.

He steps closer to me, and I realize he's been studying me all this time. He lifts my hair and pushes it behind my shoulders. He then takes my wrists, and when he wraps his hands over my fists, I see again how much bigger than me he is because my fists, they look like a child's in his giant hands.

He doesn't try to open them but sets my arms by my sides. When he touches my jaw, even though it's a featherlight touch, I flinch.

He lifts my face slowly, turns it from side to side, brushes the bruises with his knuckles, presses against them like he's fitting his fingers to the marks they left, making sure they're his. Who else?

He then slides his fingers down over my throat, cups it again, and I panic. I clasp my hand over his forearm prepared to drag him off. To fight even if it means a whipping.

But he surprises me. "I'm not going to hurt you," he says, his voice low but not harsh. Not threatening.

He could threaten. He could do so much more than threaten.

He could throw me on the bed, force my legs apart, and take what he wants.

I have no power here.

Physically, I'm no match. I am alone in this house of my enemy.

"I'm not going to hurt you," he repeats.

And I surprise myself because I feel my lip begin to tremble, feel the flush of something—God knows what—at his words because they're gentle and maybe I'm being fucking stupid but maybe I just need to believe he means them. Even if they're a lie, I need something to hold on to right now.

I let my arms drop to my sides, and when he swipes his thumb along my face and smears a tear across it, I let my lashes fall closed. He cups my face with both hands and pulls me closer.

"Look at me."

I open my eyes and look up at him. He's so close, I can see every speck of gold in his eyes and this, right now, it's like I'm more naked than if he were to look over my body, if he were to lay me out and open me up and study every detail of me.

This is worse.

This... I can't hold his gaze because this, now, him like this, it's like he's looking inside my soul.

And I'm letting him.

I blink, turn my face, meaning to look away, but

turning it into his palm and for a single insane moment, I think I am safe here. Safe in his hands, in my enemy's hands. I shake my head and with my arms, slap his off.

"You can't have that," I snap, more power in my voice than I thought I could muster.

He wipes his thumb on the corner of his mouth, like he's wiping something away. Then his eyes narrow, and I'm back against the wall. I think he knows what I mean by 'that' even though I can hardly make sense of my own words.

You can't have that.

He may be able to take my body, but he has no right to my soul.

I get the feeling he's processing the same thing because he shrugs a shoulder and makes a point of looking me over slowly, as if letting his gaze memorize every inch of skin, the rise and fall of my breasts, the concave of my belly, the mound of my sex, the curve of my thighs, the fragility of my naked feet even.

"Turn around."

I search his eyes, and they're darker, the pupils dilated.

"Why do I have to ask everything twice?" he says.

I turn, and I realize the walls are not painted. They're actually papered in a rich and very subtle paper with the most delicate pattern of roses repeating, repeating, repeating.

It's what I concentrate on when I feel his fingers on me, when I gasp at the slight touch as he gathers up my hair and sets the mass of it over my shoulder to expose my back.

I find myself resting my forehead against the wall. I wonder if the ridges of the paper will imprint their pattern on my skin. I am suddenly tired.

He's wearing me out, and he hasn't even touched me yet. Hasn't yet begun to use me.

His fingers play like a piano along my spine, tracing every vertebra as if with a feather, as if he'll know every inch of me, every centimeter.

I set my fingertips on the wall, and I trace the pattern of the roses, none of which is bigger than the fingernail of my smallest finger, and they're intertwining and suddenly overwhelming as they twist and turn their thorny, strangling stems again and again and again.

And I was wrong.

There is color.

I heard once that white contains all of the colors of the rainbow and thought what nonsense, but I see it now, in the roses that encircle this prison, my borrowed room.

I look up at it, rest the side of my cheek against the cool surface, and know there will be no reprieve, no break in the pattern. The roses are condemned to twist and turn and wind around and around and choke the life out of the next.

There will be no survivors. Not after this. Not after me.

My aunt's ring seems to burn on my finger.

"I took from them."

I look at it, meet the empty eye sockets on the tiny skull, and I know that it's not just any bone, but Scafoni bone that makes up the ring.

I shudder at the icy chill that runs up my spine.

His ancestor's bone is my jewelry, and I want to laugh.

But then he touches me, and inside my belly, a thousand butterflies take flight as his fingers brush my skin so lightly, it's almost like he doesn't. Like it's my mind playing tricks on me.

I want to turn and look to be sure, but then he cups my bottom with both hands, as if weighing or testing, perhaps for his whip, and then with one hand he gathers up my hair and for the first time in my life, I curse the length, think maybe I should cut it short, shave it like a monk, because he's twisting it around his fist.

Sebastian turns me to face him, and the fingers of his other hand are combing through the mound of hair between my legs and sliding lower.

He's hard. I feel him against my hip.

His fingers are in my folds now, and his eyes have gone black. He tilts my head back, and I hear my own shallow breathing because it feels good, what he's doing, and I don't want it to feel good, and I'm not expecting him to kiss me.

Why am I not expecting him to kiss me?

My mouth opens only because he's tugging my head backward, hurting me. I lick my lips, and I feel the warmth of his touch. He doesn't make the mistake of sliding his tongue inside my mouth. I would bite it off. Swallow it. He knows it.

Bone.

The ring is made of Scafoni bone.

He takes my lower lip between his and he's kissing me and it's so soft and erotic. His fingers between my legs have found my clit because it's swollen and sensitive and craves his touch. Like he's not my enemy at all.

When I find myself involuntarily arching my back, tilting myself into his hand, I blink my eyes open and find he's already watching me.

He's been watching me all along, the bastard.

But that's what it takes to snap me out of this insanity.

When I slap my hands on his chest to shove him away, he doesn't budge but instead closes one hand around my throat and keeps me pressed against the wall while his other hand works my clit and fuck, I can't come. I can't.

I won't.

He grins a little, like he knows my dilemma. Like he knows he'll win, and I feel my hips moving without my permission, feel myself press into his palm.

But then he makes a mistake when he kisses me again.

I close my hands over his shoulders, and I'm so close, so fucking close, and I will not give him the satisfaction of coming.

I snap my teeth and bite down hard on his lip.

The taste of blood, like iron in my mouth, it's my victory, and I swallow it and I want more, even though I know he will make me pay.

I'm grinning when he pulls back, but not for long.

He uses the fistful of my hair and tugs my head back so hard I feel like he will scalp me.

"That was a mistake."

He's pissed, and I am glad. At least he's not grinning anymore. Not smirking.

He must have known I would fight. He must want me to, because what's the fun in taking a girl who won't fight? In breaking a girl who has no fight in her?

He marches me like this, with his face inches from mine, his eyes fierce, right to the bed and tosses me roughly onto it.

His breathing is tight, like he's trying to control himself, because I'm watching his hands fist and open, fist and open, again and again.

My grin is gone now too, and I don't have a

chance to scoot away before he's on his knees on the bed and gripping my thigh with one hand—I'll have bruises like fingerprints there too, to match the ones on my jaw.

He traps my legs with his, knees pressing against my thighs, and he climbs on top of me, capturing my hands when I fight him, taking my wrists into one of his giant hands so easily.

I'm raging, screaming at him, cursing him to hell, cursing his family to hell, using every ounce of power in my body to wriggle away, to at least make him work for it, but he's just too strong and I'm no match.

I finally stop because I'm exhausted. I look up at him looming over me. He wipes his thumb across his lip and looks at it, at the smear of blood there.

"That was a fucking mistake."

"You have no right to touch me. To kiss me. Let me go!"

"After I've been so patient with you."

"Patient?"

"You don't get it."

He takes the hand with the smear of blood on it and tugs at the mound of hair between my legs, and it fucking hurts.

"You belong to me," he says.

He must be making a fist with his hand because he's pulling so hard.

"You're hurting me!" I'm powerless to move, to make him stop.

"I haven't begun hurting you," he says as he moves his fingers, giving me a moment of relief before he slides them lower and grips my pussy hard, digging his fingers inside me.

I make a sound, a whine, a moan. I don't fucking know.

"You belong to me, Helena. I am your master. I decide when you eat, if you eat. I decide when or if you sleep and in whose bed. I decide if you're allowed clothes. I decide if you'll scrub my floors. I decide everything. Me. I am your fucking master."

"Stop. Please." It comes out a plea, and I hate myself for it, for the tears sliding out of my eyes. For being afraid of him. Of him like this.

"I decide when you're rewarded, and I decide when you're punished. And I should warn you, I have a taste for the latter and you're already owed. More than once."

I swallow, and I'm squirming like a tiny animal, helpless. Like a fucking rabbit caught in a trap.

"I own you, body and soul."

"No. Not soul. Not that."

He pulls his hand from my pussy, and I can breathe again.

He brings it to his nose, and his smile grows so fucking wide, I want to kill him. To smash his perfect teeth in, his perfect face, and I feel myself burn with humiliation when he smears his wet fingers rudely across my face, my mouth.

I smell my scent, that of arousal above all else. He smells it too, and he wants me to know it.

"You have sharp teeth and a sharper tongue, but I'll break you of those. I'll make better use of your mouth, like I will your pussy and your ass because I own every hole. And you will know that you are nothing. Nothing but my fuck toy. And you know what else, Helena? I'll take the greatest pleasure watching you come. Watching you as you realize your body will betray you. Your pussy will betray you. It already has."

"I hate you. I'll fight you."

He brings his face to mine, and that grin is still there.

"And therein lies the reason it was you and not your meek Barbie doll sisters."

He sits up, squeezes his thighs around mine one last time, then gets up off the bed.

I remain as I am, lying there, spent, every muscle on fire like I've just run a fucking marathon.

But then he draws my pocketknife out of his pocket and opens the blade.

"So I'll give you a notch for that little stunt."

He catches me by the hair, drags me to my knees on the floor, and turns my face into the bed, pushing it into the mattress and holding me there by my hair.

I feel the sharp tip of the blade at the back of my

neck, I let out a cry and grip the blanket, pulling hard.

"Be still. You don't want me to slip up."

It stings, every centimeter of the cut. He's carving a line into the back of my neck.

Warm blood runs down my spine. I hold still, like he says.

"There," he says, releasing me.

"What did you do?" I touch my neck, and my fingers come away bloodied.

He looks at the blade, wipes it clean with his finger, closes it, and tucks it into his pocket.

"I like it when you fight, Helena. I want you to fight. To run. To try to hurt me."

He glances at his forearm, where tracks of skin are missing from where I scratched it off, and I suddenly am very aware of it under my fingernails.

He looks back at me. "Because it's so much more fun when I have to make you."

"You mean when you rape me?"

His jaw tightens. He wasn't expecting that. I know he's gritting his teeth. I've touched a nerve.

"And then pass me on to your brothers to rape me?" I continue.

"Be careful."

"Isn't that what you do? Isn't that the point? You take a Willow Girl, and you beat her and you rape her, and you break her so that when you return her, she's already dead even if you don't kill her."

I sag against the bed, and I'm not fighting anymore. There isn't any more fight in my voice, because that last part, I didn't mean to say that out loud. Not for his sake, but my own. Because with those words, I've just read my own death sentence.

He's quiet for a long minute, just stands there and watches me wipe the stupid fucking tears from my eyes. When he steps toward the bed, I lean away, but he stops, doesn't reach for me, doesn't touch me.

"You want to keep your soul? I'm not interested in your soul. But don't fucking push me. I am your only ally in this house. Remember that."

I snort. "My ally?"

"Now get up and clean yourself up. Have a shower. Lunch will be sent up in twenty minutes, and the doctor will be here at two o'clock."

"What?"

He walks to the door and only stops once he has opened it.

"What doctor?" I ask.

How many humiliations can he put me through? We were all checked already, my sisters and I, to make sure we were *intact*, as the doctor called it. Virgins. He knows I'm not. He knew it when he chose me.

"Birth control. I won't father a Willow Girl."

5

HELENA

"*I won't father a Willow Girl.*"

My mind is spinning. What is this? What is happening?

Sebastian's gone. He closed the door behind him, but I didn't hear a lock turn. Not too reassuring, though, because if he doesn't feel the need to lock the door, he isn't worried I'll run. And I won't. The punishment wouldn't be mine if I did.

It would be my family's.

I get up off the bed, pick up my discarded blanket, and go into the bathroom. Turning my back to the mirror, I lift my hair and look at the wound. It's about two inches long but shallow.

I run the water and wash my hands, wash his skin out from underneath my fingernails before using a washcloth to clean up the blood, then look through the medicine cabinet where, remarkably, I find a first-aid kit. After I've cleaned and dressed the wound, I go back into the bedroom and walk over to the window.

Venice. He'd said we were going to Venice.

But I stand here in awe as I look out of my window on the second floor of the house, and I don't see Venice like I imagined it. I see land and water.

I push the windows out and am surprised that I can open them. They must not be afraid I'll jump, at least not yet. I lean my head out, and in every direction that I can see from here, there is only land and water.

No city. No gondolas. No sound of a thousand tourists.

The grass is green, and it's well-groomed. There are two gardeners in the distance. To the right of the house is what looks to be a vegetable garden. To the left, I see the dock where three boats bob in the water. They're wooden and look like the elegant water taxis I've seen in photos of Venice.

Strange thing is, I've always wanted to see Venice. I've always been enamored of it. There's a mystery, something unique and belonging only to this city.

But this—this is not what I imagined and not what I know Venice proper to look like.

There's a knock on my door.

I turn as it opens. I don't know who I expect it'll be, as I don't see Sebastian or any of them knocking. I breathe a sigh of relief when I see it's a girl with a tray. She's probably around my age, and she gives me a little nod before setting the tray down on the larger table by the chaise. She then turns to leave without a word.

"Wait," I call out just when she reaches the door. I feel ridiculous hugging this blanket to myself and chasing her down.

She turns but is visibly uncomfortable.

"Where are we? This isn't Venice."

She looks behind her into the hallway, squeezes her lips together, wrings her hands.

Maybe she doesn't speak English, and I don't speak Italian.

"Venezia?" I think that's how it's said in Italian.

She looks down at her feet, like she's thinking about something, then looks up, nods, and rushes from the room. And I get the feeling she wasn't nervous because of the language.

She wasn't allowed to talk to me. Is anyone? Or will I be completely isolated? Wholly alone?

I shove the thought aside and go over to the tray, stumbling a little when the blanket gets caught between my feet. I gather it up and look at what's for lunch. My stomach growls. I am hungry and missed breakfast.

I do wonder if I was drugged because I don't know how I slept through landing and being carried in here and stripped naked. But why drug me? What's the point? There's no need.

There are two pots, and I lift the lid off each one. One is coffee and the other tea. Is that because they weren't sure what I prefer?

No, it's not a kindness. I should remember that.

I pour myself a cup of coffee and add a generous helping of cream. It's good, although much stronger than I'm used to.

I take off the top piece of ciabatta from the sandwich and find inside roasted vegetables and goat cheese with pine nuts and what I guess is a pesto sauce. It looks good and I'm hungry, so I set the coffee down and pick up the sandwich with one hand while holding up my blanket with the other and take a bite.

My mouth full, I go to one of the other two doors I haven't yet investigated.

One is locked, so I turn to the next one. It's a huge walk-in closet, but it's empty.

How long does he plan on keeping me naked?

There's no clock in the room, and I wonder how much time has passed. I quickly eat the rest of the sandwich and drink my coffee before going into the bathroom to have a shower.

I have the quickest shower I've ever had. I know any of them can walk in at any time, and I'm vulnerable enough without being caught naked in the shower.

When I'm finished, I grab two towels, make a turban for my hair with one and wrap the other around myself—it's a little wieldier than the long blanket. I towel dry my hair and leave that towel hanging on a rack.

Just as I return to the bedroom, that door opens and Lucinda Scafoni walks inside followed by a man too old to still be walking, along with the same girl who brought my tray. She pushes an empty metal table on wheels inside, doesn't dare look at me, but curtsies to Lucinda and leaves. When she reaches to close the door behind her, Lucinda stops her.

"Leave it open," she says in English, all the while watching me with distaste.

She's wearing a black dress with a collar that reaches to the top of her neck. It's severe and ugly. Her hair is, again, in a tight bun, and I see now how her makeup is too heavy. The powder is caked over a thick layer of foundation, her eyebrows, if they existed once, are long gone. She's drawn them in, and they're too dark. Too stark. Even with her olive coloring.

I don't think she was ever beautiful.

"Take off the towel," she orders me, and I notice she's carrying a long, thin stick in her hand.

"Why?"

I hug the towel tighter as I try to keep her gaze, but from my periphery, I watch the doctor lay out his things, hear the soft clank of metal on metal. Recognize the instruments.

"I've already had an exam," I say.

"You'll have another. Take off the towel."

"Where's Sebastian?" Why do I ask?

"He asked me to take care of this chore."

I stop at that.

He asked her to take care of this?

But what did I think? That he'd save me? God, I'm a bigger fool than I realize if that's truly what I think.

"If you don't take off the towel, I will ask Ethan to come and remove it from you."

I swallow. I know she means it. I unwrap the towel and drop it to the floor.

The doctor is still working on unpacking his things or at least he has the courtesy not to look up, but she looks me up and down, up and down.

"Turn."

I do.

"Not a mark on you."

"All the Willow Girls have perfect, beautiful skin," I taunt, turning back to face her, because I think I understand at least some of her hate for me. For all the Willow Girls.

But she grins. "Makes it that much more gratifying to mark an unscarred, arrogant whore." She points to the bed. "Lie down and open your legs."

"I've already had my exam, and Sebastian said this was for birth control." But then again, he already betrayed me, didn't he?

But is it betrayal when he is my enemy? No, not at all. His behavior is in keeping with his role.

"I need to be sure you're not diseased. He should have taken one of your sisters. I don't like the idea of my sons fucking a used Willow whore."

"It's not necessary. I'm clean."

I've had sex exactly once for the sole purpose of ripping through that membrane. And look where it got me.

"Ethan."

She doesn't even look away and, as if he were standing right outside, Ethan appears in the doorway. I can't scoop up the towel fast enough.

"Help her," she tells him.

Sebastian is punishing me. This is what I get for standing up to him. This is all a part of that breaking.

"No." I keep the towel around me but sit on the bed. "He can go. I'll do it." Lying back to prove my point.

"Open the towel," she instructs.

I'd kept it wrapped around me.

Looking up at the ceiling, I open it.

"Now open your legs."

"Ethan can leave. I'll do it."

"You'll do it regardless."

Ethan steps to the foot of the bed. I guess he wants a front-row seat.

I glance once at his mother and know it's pointless to ask again, and I won't beg. I open my legs. The doctor says something to Mrs. Scafoni in Italian, and she kindly translates.

"Pull your knees up."

I do. And I'm wholly exposed to them, and all I can do is lie there and stare up at the ceiling and fist the bedsheets as the doctor conducts his examination, the instruments he pushes inside me cold, his old fingers poking me and just when I think we're done, he's given another instruction I don't understand, not until I watch him smear lubricant onto his thickest finger and poke at my other hole and when I tighten up, it's Ethan who speaks.

"It's easier to take something up your ass when you're relaxed," he says. "And what I'm going to put in there will be much thicker than the doctor's finger."

Is this part of Sebastian's punishment? This utter humiliation, this being taken down about a hundred notches?

My face burns as the doctor pushes his finger inside me. I don't understand the point, but there isn't one. It's to humiliate me, that's all. And he does. And when he's done, I'm given a shot. The birth control, I guess.

When it's over, he stands and takes off his gloves. Mrs. Scafoni approaches and, her eyes on me, has a discussion in Italian with the doctor. A moment later, the same girl who rolled in the cart returns and rolls it out. I reach for the towel.

"Roll over onto your stomach."

I glance from her to Ethan, who is grinning, his hand on the erection evident through his jeans. I swear he's not right.

"Why?"

"Ethan."

She doesn't even entertain my question, and I roll onto my stomach before he can lay his hands on me.

A second later, before I can process the whooshing sound, a line of fire burns across my ass, has me gasping, jumping from the bed.

But Ethan pounces, and I'm desperately covering myself as he roughly grabs hold of me, dragging me back down.

"You're owed three more for your refusal to do as you're told," Lucinda informs me. "He can hold you down, and I'll double it, or you can submit on your own and take the three. Decide."

"What refusal? I did what you said!"

"That's another strike. Ethan."

I shake my head, but I know Lucinda won't give me another chance. She likes this too much, and Ethan too, and I watch, helpless, as two cuffs, attached to the headboard, are exposed.

"No!"

But he, like his brother, is too strong, and my

arms are bound and I'm on my belly and he takes hold of my ankles and has me stretched tight.

"Eight more since I'm doubling. Next time, you'll know to submit immediately."

And with that, I receive the first caning of my life, because that's what the stick she's holding is. A fucking cane.

Only once growing up did my parents lay a hand on me, but this pain, it's different. Eight strokes in addition to the one and I'm sobbing by the second, sobbing and begging her to stop, hating her, hating myself, wondering how something can hurt so badly, wondering if she's ripping through skin. Wondering if Sebastian ordered this too.

When she's finished, she's out of breath. Ethan releases my legs. I don't turn to look at them. I bury my face in my arm instead.

"She should take care of this," I hear Ethan say to her.

I don't know what he's talking about, but then his mother answers, and I think I do, I'm sickened.

"Soon enough. Get one of the girls from the kitchen for now," Lucinda says.

I hear him leave. The bed depresses, and sharp fingernails scratch along my buttock, touching every line she just whipped into me, before combing into my hair, pushing it from my face.

I don't want to look at her. I can see her victorious grin in the periphery of my blurry vision.

But she takes my hair in one hand and pulls my head back, turns it painfully, so I have to look at her.

"You're pretty, but so was your predecessor when she came here."

I know she means my Aunt Libby, but I didn't realize Lucinda was here during her turn as the Willow Girl.

The Willow Whipping Girl.

"She was pretty too, in the beginning. Tell me, did you see her back when she returned to you?"

"Her back?"

She grins. "My husband gave me the chore of punishing that whore."

Her husband? Sebastian's father? He was married to Lucinda when he took my aunt?

"I look forward to the same with you."

With that, she gets up. I watch her walk out the door, leaving me bound, lying on my bed.

Did I think she'd be different than the sons? Because she is a woman? I saw her cruelty from the first I saw her, and her hatred of me, of my family, is almost palpable.

Again, I wish I knew more of our history. Wish my mother had told us more. Wish I'd read more.

I roll to my back but quickly turn back onto my stomach. At least the pain gets me out of my head. My heart's frantic beating is finally slowing, but the pain of my punishment only seems to intensify, making my skin throb, and all I can think about is what Sebastian said to me. That he is my master, and he decides my rewards and my punishments.

And then the other thing he said.

"I am your only ally in this house. Remember that."

My ally.

My ally ordered this? Then I'm finished.

6

SEBASTIAN

I return to the house under an almost pink glow. The sunsets this time of year are spectacular. I needed to be in Venice proper for a meeting, and the timing was good. I had to walk away from her before I did something rash.

But being away didn't keep that one word, her accusation, from repeating in my head again and again and again.

Rape.

Although is it so extraordinary for her to use that word? I know what the Scafoni family is capable of. Is culpable of.

What is it you intend to do? asks the voice inside my head yet again.

I don't answer that. Instead, I divert to what my brother would already have done if he stood in my place. I know it's a cop-out, a diversion. I'm only fooling myself.

He'll still have his chance. They both will.

I shove that thought roughly away. There's time before that. Before handing her over to them.

I feel older than my twenty-eight years. I've been head of this family for ten years. I came of age years after my father's death, and I know my obligations. I know the cost if I fail to continue the tradition. As archaic as it is, there is truth to the curse. The shadow of the family mausoleum in the far distance of the property stands as a constant reminder.

Remy, the caretaker of the house and a man I trust, meets me at the dock as I step out of the boat. He's older, in his late sixties, and has been working for my family longer than I've been alive. He takes the ropes and a moment later, the boat is secured.

"How are things here?"

I can see from his face that something is wrong.

"The doctor came and went."

Remy knows about the business of the Willow Girl. Helena will be his second.

"What is it?" I push.

"The girl is still in her room. No food has been sent up. No water. Not since lunchtime."

"And she hasn't come downstairs?"

"Mrs. Scafoni forbade anyone entering, and, I assume, leaving."

I narrow my eyes, take in a slow breath. "Thank you, Remy."

He nods, ever elegant, and I head to the house.

The lights are lit in most of the downstairs rooms, but I don't see any of my family as I make my way directly up the stairs and to Helena's room.

I don't knock but push it open to find her lying on the bed on her stomach, naked. I know her arms are bound because she can't be comfortable having them over her head like that.

She doesn't stir, and I assume she's sleeping. Her hair is wild, covering her arms and most of her back, but when I step nearer, I see the marks on her ass and I fist my hands.

I go to her, study each of the nine lines of the cane. Nine strokes. Nine fucking strokes.

I didn't order this. Not like this.

But I knew Lucinda would show no mercy, didn't I? Her hatred of the Willow Girls surpasses all of ours. I know why, at least in part. I stood witness to it all when the last one was here.

Still, this?

I don't excuse it. Lucinda will need to be dealt with.

I sit on the edge of the bed. Helena stirs as I reach over to unbind her. She lets out a groan and draws her arms down, turns onto her side, and flinches. She lies back on her stomach.

She pushes the hair from her face. It's puffy from

crying, and when I meet her dark gaze, what I see inside makes my jaw tighten, makes my hands fist again.

"You're my only ally in this house?" she asks, wiping her face, forcing herself to roll onto her side, biting down on the pain. "Then what will I do when my enemies strike?"

I get up, go into the bathroom. I run cold water and drench a towel in it, then return to the bedroom.

"Turn on your stomach."

"Why? For more? Or so you can gawk?"

"This will cool it."

She snorts.

"Turn on your stomach, Helena."

"What, not Willow Girl? Not sweetheart?"

I meet her eyes, realize I hadn't called her either. "I didn't order this."

"No? That's not what your mother said."

"I didn't order the caning. Not like this."

"Not like this?" she asks. She turns her face away, like she's embarrassed.

I see the skin of her forehead crease as she wipes the back of her hand across her face. She turns on her stomach, and I lay the cool towel over the red-striped flesh of her bottom.

"Like what, then? What did you order, exactly?"

"One stroke. Two at most. Not nine."

"One stroke. Two at most. So casual about beating a woman."

I feel my lips tighten into a line, but she's right, isn't she? This, nine strokes, what would I call it?

I see the tray of food from earlier and go to it, pour a glass of water, and carry it back to the bed.

"Here."

She looks at it, then at me, and pushes herself up to take the cup. She won't let me help her to drink it. She takes a sip then hands it back.

"Are you hungry?"

"I just want to be alone." She lays her head down, closes her eyes.

"Helena—"

"Just leave me alone!" she snaps, lifting her head, glaring at me. "Can't you give me that? One night. One night after this. Please." Her voice breaks, and I see her face crumple before she turns it away from me. I swallow over the lump in my throat when I listen to her quietly sob.

I stand.

"I'll have some food sent up. Something for the pain too."

She doesn't reply, and I guess I'm not sure what she'd say.

I leave her alone, as she requested, and make sure someone takes dinner up to her before finding my family gathered at the table outside, my stepmother sitting in my chair at the head of the table.

When I get there, she's grinning, casually sipping

champagne. Ethan too. Gregory is unreadable, as usual.

"Lucinda."

They all turn to me, and whatever she sees on my face wipes that smile right off hers. She gets up, takes her chair at the foot of the table.

"Son," she says once she's seated, knowing how I hate her calling me her son because I am not. "Pour me more champagne." She holds out her glass.

I go to the table, take the bottle, and pour. "What are you celebrating?"

"Our new Willow Girl." She raises her glass and drinks a long swallow.

I grip her by the throat, and Ethan is on his feet an instant later when she spills her refilled glass of champagne onto his lap the moment I take hold of her.

Because seeing Helena like that, well, I know what Lucinda is capable of. What she can do with that cane. I grew up on the receiving end of it and have the scars to prove it.

"If you ever touch her like that again, I will kill you, do you understand me?" I squeeze her tiny, scrawny neck, and she's gripping my forearm, trying to drag me off.

"Am. I. Clear?" I ask once more, loosening my hold enough so she can choke out an answer.

"Yes!"

"Good." I release her, and she stumbles backward.

"I didn't break precious Willow skin. I only did what you asked."

"She deserved it, Sebastian. The girl is arrogant, like mama says. She taunted mama," Ethan says.

Rage turns my vision black for a second.

Gregory chuckles, and I think I hear him calling Ethan an idiot under his breath.

I shoot Gregory a look. He knows I don't like that.

"You were there?" I turn my attention to Ethan.

He clears his throat, wavers, glances at Lucinda for direction.

"Did you lay a hand on her, Ethan?" I'm trying to rein in my rage, at least with him.

"No," Ethan answers, panicked. I know I need to go easy on him. He can't control his emotions, and that's not his fault.

"Ethan did nothing wrong. Even though he has as much right to that little whore as you."

"No, he doesn't. Not yet."

"I just looked. I didn't touch her, Sebastian. I didn't."

Fuck.

I sit down, raise my eyebrows as one of the girls from the kitchen puts a whiskey down for me.

"What did I ask you to do, exactly, *stepmother*?" She hates being called that. She may hate it more than when I call her by her first name. But she will answer because she alone is the one responsible.

Her lips purse. "She should learn on her first punishment that disobedience will cost her."

"What did I ask you to do exactly?" I repeat, draining my glass. The girl refills it.

"The examination."

And this is true. I did want her re-examined for the simple reason of bringing her down a notch. "And?"

"She disobeyed, like we all knew she would."

"How many did I order if she disobeyed?"

"One or two strokes."

"And you delivered?"

"I didn't break skin!"

"How many strokes did you deliver?"

"You saw for yourself. And if you want her to respect you, you'll deliver nine more now. That will teach her."

"That will break her."

"Isn't that the point?" she hisses.

"On my timeline, Lucinda, not yours. She belongs to me. You do as I dictate to the fucking letter, or you'll be the one on the post. Are we clear?"

Her left eye twitches. It always does when she wants to tell someone to go fuck themselves.

"Are we clear?" I repeat, my face stone.

"Yes."

"Good. Now get out of my sight."

It takes her a minute, and I know she's cursing me to hell and back, but I don't care.

She walks into the house as the servers bring out dinner: a roast chicken with potatoes, vegetables and a salad.

I look at Ethan as I chew my first bite of chicken.

"You should have stopped her."

He looks at me. "I didn't want to, and when it's my turn, I won't."

"It's not your turn yet, brother. You stay away from the girl, or I'll be angry with you, understand?"

"Mama says I get to have her too. She says you want to keep her all to yourself. But I get my turn too." He eats a forkful of chicken, washes it down with a swallow of wine.

"How did the meeting go?" Gregory asks, sitting back in his seat.

I don't know if he's uninterested in Helena or what. Maybe he's just smart enough to keep his head down because he has two years to wait.

Hell, maybe he's smart enough to know that between Lucinda, Ethan and me, there may not be much left when his turn comes at all.

The meeting was with our bankers. I confirmed the first installment of the payment that should be sent to the Willow family and looked over everyone's accounts. I need to keep a tight rein over Lucinda and Ethan, because even if Helena is bound to be handed over to him after my year is up, I still control the family funds. It's how I plan to keep control of him when he has her.

I wonder how much Helena knows about the money that exchanges hands after the reaping and through the years the Willow Girl is property of the Scafoni family. I wonder how she'd feel about her own precious family if she did know.

"Good," I say, glancing at Ethan. "Things are on track."

After dinner, we all go our separate ways, Gregory leaving the island for some party or other, Ethan retiring to his room. I go for a walk, making my way to the east side of the island where the Scafoni Family Mausoleum is.

This path is not lighted, and I swear the grass here is browner. Nothing grows here anymore, like the ashes of the dead infect the earth here with death. It's always cooler on this side of the island too, and that makes no scientific sense.

This is why some part of me goes along with this insane business of the Willow Girls.

I don't believe in any god, but I do believe in ghosts. I believe those of the Willows are vengeful, but more so, I believe in the curse Maggie Scafoni, Anabelle's mother, placed on us centuries ago.

Sometimes, the women of our family can be as fierce as the men because twice, a Willow Girl wasn't claimed. Two generations that let the past lie, that allowed conscience to rule over family tradition and obligation.

That's when the Scafoni family began to lose their firstborn sons, the loss leading to infighting among us because it changed the rules of inheritance.

Breaking with the tradition and displeasing our ancestors cost us.

After that, whether a Willow Girl was claimed or not, each generation lost one boy—some during pregnancy, some within days of birth. Always the first, so rather than having four sons, each family had only three.

The soft light of a lamp burns inside the mausoleum day and night, three hundred and sixty-five days a year, like the sanctuary lamp on every altar in every Christian church.

I push the creaky gate back and step inside. I don't use my phone to shine more light on the space. I don't need it, and I'm not afraid of these ghosts. They are here, yes, but they don't mean harm. Not to me.

It's big, the family's final resting place, and will need to be expanded soon. The walls are already filled up.

I go to the freshest one, that of my father. I trace the dates. He died young, in his early fifties. He was not an unkind man, not to us at least, but he was weak.

The canings didn't start until Lucinda was in the picture. She declared herself the disciplinarian—at least my disciplinarian. I swear, as sick as it is, she got a kick out of it.

I endured her wrath through my seventeenth year. I was a man, yet I endured her punishments until I couldn't stand another minute of her hate.

I remember the last time she ordered me to strip. I remember my rage. I broke her damned cane in two that night and dragged her to the whipping post.

Never again did she raise a finger to me, raise her voice to me, or dare disobey me.

Not until now.

I think about my mother. I was two years old when she died, but I remember her being kind and gentle. I remember loving her.

How Lucinda could be so different from my mother, I don't understand. They share blood and yet, they're like night and day.

The memory of the marks on Helena make me remember the times we were made to watch Lucinda punish the last Willow Girl, Libby. What she endured at Lucinda's hands makes me sick. But what makes me sicker is that my father was too weak to stop her, even though I know in his own way, he loved Libby Willow.

Maybe that's why Lucinda hated her so much and punished her so harshly.

I have to take care with Helena. I can't allow

Lucinda to do to her what she did to Libby. I don't have any interest in being her savior, but I will be the one to break her, not Lucinda.

I step to the right, to the next name carved in the black marble. To the dates there.

Timothy Scafoni. Older than me by thirteen minutes. He lived three days. My mother had thought the curse had been broken, and in a way, it had. She had twins—there were no other twins in the Scafoni line—and I survived.

Beside my brother's marker is that of my mother, Samantha. I brush dust off the stone and rub the engraving of her name. It's been a long time since she died.

I take three of the candles lying nearby, light them, and set them in front of each of the markers. Then, without a word of prayer, I walk back out of the mausoleum and to the house.

7

HELENA

When I wake in the morning, I'm surprised to find the curtains drawn closed. I hadn't gotten up after Sebastian left. Every time I woke up, I just closed my eyes again, still hoping, like a coward, that this was a dream. Still hoping the next time I opened my eyes, I'd be in my own house, in my own bed.

I slowly sit up, pushing through the pain because I have to use the bathroom. I make myself sit on the edge of the bed, in fact. Make myself feel the sting of my first beating at the hands of a Scafoni because I don't ever want to forget the cruelty, the brutality of this family.

Lucinda Scafoni dished out my punishment with pleasure. It was no chore to cane me.

I think about Aunt Libby, wonder at what she

went through. I think about what Lucinda asked me, if I'd seen my aunt's back.

I was five when she came back home from her 'trip,' and my memories are clouded, but the image of her back I've never forgotten. The day I saw them, she was coming out of the shower when I'd burst into her room, surprising her. I remember asking her about the patterns on her back, asking if they were a tattoo because I'd never seen anything like it.

She didn't have a chance to answer me because my mother swept into the room and carried me out, chastising me that I shouldn't walk into someone's room without knocking. Now I know why.

On the nightstand is a pot of cream. I pick it up, open it, sniff it, and read the label. It's a cooling cream. For my ass, I guess.

I put it down, more annoyed than grateful because when you order a punishment, you don't get to be forgiven with a pathetic attempt to lessen the pain. I won't ever forgive Sebastian for what he did.

I get up and go into the bathroom. The first thing I do is turn my back to the mirror and look at myself, look at the damage, and I gasp.

Nine angry red lines mark my bottom, all in a tight, neat row. She has a practiced hand. The skin is bruised in places, turning blue, but those lines, they're a bright red. I reach back to feel the skin. It's raised and tender to the touch. I'll feel this for the next few days or even weeks.

I haven't washed myself since the exam. I climb into the shower and turn the water on. I keep it as cold as I can stand because hot stings. Like yesterday, I don't take my time. I used to. I always found it a pleasure to take long showers, use up all the hot water. My sisters always complained.

The memory makes me smile. I miss them. I wonder if he'll let me have any contact with them or with Aunt Helena. Maybe he'll feel badly enough that he'll say yes if I ask today.

When I go back into the bedroom, there's a knock on the door. It opens. The same girl from yesterday walks in, and we both blush. She knows what they did to me. She witnessed my humiliation. For a moment, I wonder if she was the girl Ethan used to relieve himself.

God, I think I'd be sick if I had anything in my stomach.

She sets the tray of food down and clears the old one. I guess Sebastian had had dinner sent, but I hadn't even noticed.

"Thank you."

She nods, offers a warm smile, and leaves. I pour myself a cup of coffee and notice they didn't bring tea this time. I eat all three croissants, one plain, two chocolate. I'm starving. I then take the bunch of grapes and go to the window, push it open, and watch outside while I pop one after another into my mouth.

When the door opens without a knock, I startle and turn to find Sebastian walking inside. I stiffen and hold my towel against myself, finding it hard to swallow the last grape.

He looks at me and gives me a brief smile. He's carrying boxes, one large with a pink bow on it, the other smaller. A shoe box, I think.

"Good morning."

"Is it?"

"How do you feel?"

I give a fake smile. "Peachy."

He sets the boxes on the bed. "I brought you a dress to wear today. And there's more on the way."

"Is that because you feel guilty?"

"Are you always like this?"

"Like what?"

"Difficult. Confrontational."

"I guess that's what your mother thought to cane out of me."

He stiffens. "Lucinda's been dealt with. She crossed a line, but it won't happen again."

Again, he refers to her as Lucinda. It's strange. "Am I supposed to be grateful? I mean, after all, you did sic her on me to begin with."

He crosses the room and just stops short of taking hold of my arm. I can see the effort it takes him to control himself.

His gaze falls to my chest, and I hug the towel to me.

"Let me clarify," he says, meeting my eyes again. "It won't happen again without my order, Willow Girl."

Willow Girl.

That puts me in my place.

I study him, hear the warning in his tone.

He doesn't feel guilty. He's not upset. He *dealt* with it, whatever the hell that means. I'm the one who'll deal with the bruised ass, not to mention the bruised ego.

"Go to hell."

"I'm going to let that one go, considering. Get dressed and come downstairs. You have five minutes," he says, turning toward the door.

"Why?" I push, although my voice is lower, and I half-expect him to not hear me. But he stops with one foot in the hallway. "Why are you giving me clothes?"

"Because I don't want everyone gawking at what's mine."

Ah. What's his.

Property.

What did I expect?

"Five minutes. I'm waiting at the bottom of the stairs."

He leaves with that and, after taking a deep, steadying breath—because this man pulls the rug out from under me like no one else—I take the lid off the smaller of the two boxes to find a pair of slingback sandals inside. They're white with a tiny heel. I recognize the brand from my sister's magazines. Designer.

I check the size and am surprised to find he got it right.

I pull on the large bow and open the bigger box, pushing the scented pink tissue paper aside to find a turquoise sundress inside. It has a halter top and is cut low on the back. The skirt ends midthigh in a ruffle. It's pretty, very pretty, and I'm glad it's not formfitting.

When I slip it on, though, I realize it shows off enough without needing to be. It doesn't allow for a bra—and even if it did, I don't have one. My breasts are a very modest B cup at their most full time of the month, and this sort of dress is new for me. I'd never wear it at home.

The fabric is softest cotton. A glance in the mirror shows me it's not see-through. I slip on the sandals, and the look is soft. Very feminine. The turquoise complements my skin and hair.

I peek under the tissue paper for underwear, but there doesn't seem to be any. Which is probably for the best, since I don't think I could wear any today anyway.

Back in the bathroom, I brush out my hair and set it over my shoulders. I need to ask him for some clips or hair ties or something. I'm used to my hair pulled off my face and neck, especially in the summer.

Guessing I took just over the five minutes I was allotted, I open the door and, for the first time, step into the hallway. I look right and left and up. There's another level to the house, and this floor houses, from what I can see, seven rooms. I'm not sure if one is a linen closet or bathroom, maybe laundry. All of the doors are closed.

Our house back home is big too. It's been in the family for generations. But, opposite this house, it's old and needs repair with whole sections closed off, and it's always too cold in winter and too hot in summer.

I take a few steps, and I'm at the top of the wide, opulent staircase. Sebastian is downstairs. I can see him in what I guess is the living room, and he's on his phone. I make my way down. He looks up at me when he hears my heels clicking on the stairs.

When I reach the first floor, I look around as he wraps up his call. Large living room on one side, larger dining room to the other with a long, rectangular table that looks like it can seat more than a dozen people.

French doors lead outside from each room, making the space bright.

The front doors are opulent, the wood light in color, the carving intricate, each door making up one half of the giant symbol drawn in it with two smaller ones on either bottom corner.

Sebastian comes to me, and I watch him look me over, nod in approval. He's dressed casually, wearing jeans and T-shirt, same as yesterday. Again, I see the tattoos. It takes me a minute to drag my eyes away.

I clear my throat at the awkward moment.

"What is that?" I ask, pointing to the door.

"Scafoni family crest."

"Wow. Is that in case you accidentally walk up to the wrong house?"

He smiles, puts his hand at my low back, and the contact of skin on skin sends a small current of electricity sparking through me. It's instantaneous and quick, and I wonder if he feels it at all.

"No chance of that. We're the only house on the island."

Island. Wow. They own a freaking island.

"I thought we were in Venice."

"We are. This is Isola Anabelle, one of Venice's islands."

"Oh." I sound stupid, I know, but honestly, I'd never thought about anything but Venice proper when I thought about Venice.

"This is the living room. You're welcome in here anytime. Dining room, same thing. Although I advise you to stay in your room when I'm not on the property."

"Because you're my only ally?"

He narrows his eyes, gives me a smile that warns me to watch myself, and continues. "Any doors that are closed on any level are off-limits. Don't let me catch you inside any of them."

I face him, meet his charcoal gaze. He must have shaved this morning because it's the first time I've seen him without scruff along his jaw.

"Or you'll send your mommy to cane me?" I can't help asking, even though I know I shouldn't.

"Nah," he says, leaning in close, tucking a strand of hair behind my ear. He's studying me as closely as I am him. I wonder what he sees. "I'll cane you myself."

His hand is at my elbow, fingers closing around it.

A shudder runs through me, and I don't know if it's his breath at my neck or the words themselves that do it. I look up at him, swallow, my smile fading as his grows.

"You won't win with me, Helena."

"I won't give up without a fight, Sebastian."

"Choose your battles wisely, then, or you'll wear yourself out before we've even arrived on the battlefield."

"We arrived on the battlefield the moment I was made to step onto the block to be poked and prodded as if I were cattle."

"If you're not careful, it won't be a block I put you on."

I stop, no comeback, his words from yesterday too fresh in my mind.

He's referring to the whipping post.

Someone clears their throat, and Sebastian's hand squeezes my elbow. "Helena, this is Remy. He's a sort of butler. If you need something and can't find me, you find him, understand?"

I turn to Sebastian, and I feel like he means more than he's saying.

"Is he my ally too?" I ask.

"You're wearing on me," he says, introducing me to Remy, who smiles and bows.

He then walks me toward a swinging door that opens up into a very large kitchen. Blue-and-white tiles cover every wall, and there is a wood-burning stove where flatbread is puffing as it bakes.

The counters look to be concrete and very modern, like the appliances, and there's a huge island where a cook is standing over the cooktop, stirring a pot. The scent coming from it makes my mouth water.

She's older and has her gray hair tied back into a bun. She wipes her hands on the apron around her ample hips and nods her greeting.

"This is Miriam. She's our cook."

"Nice to meet you," I say, stepping closer to peek into the pot. "What is it?" I ask, even though I don't want to appear interested in anything he has to show me.

She answers in Italian and, while he translates, dips a spoon into the broth and holds it out for me to taste. She makes a motion for me to blow on it, and I like her already.

"Stock for tonight's soup," Sebastian says. "It's vegetarian. You're a vegetarian, right?"

I glance at him, taken aback. "Yes. And it's delicious," I say, directing that last part to Miriam, who smiles proudly.

I don't thank him for accommodating my diet.

"I'll let you know where you'll take your meals each day. If you miss a meal, you wait until the next one. Remember that."

"Don't skip meals, or I'll be sent to bed without my supper. Got it."

He smiles, and his hand grips my arm a little too tightly.

I follow him through the open door and into the bright sunshine. I stand in it for a minute, enjoying its rays, its warmth. From here, I can see in the distance that one of the three boats is gone. He follows my gaze.

"My family is off the island for the day."

I turn to him. "When you said you dealt with your mother, what does that mean?"

"It means she'll think twice about hurting you again. And to clarify, she's my stepmother."

Stepmother?

But before I can ask more, he's guiding me away again.

"This way."

We walk along the property, and I'm in awe. I've never seen something so serenely beautiful as Isola Anabelle. The grass is lush, the water surrounding it—the Adriatic, I believe—quiet and blue.

There's a swimming pool that is calling to me. With three sisters, swimming was my time to be alone. It's my haven, being beneath the surface. The pool is Olympic-size, and comfortable lounge chairs are situated along the circumference.

"Where is Venice proper?"

"About a fifteen-minute boat ride away."

"And there's no one else on this island but your family and the staff?"

"Correct."

"Do they live here too, the staff?"

"Yes. That building there houses them." He points to a smaller replica of the house, the stonework as beautiful as the main house, nestled in what appears to be a small outcrop of trees.

We turn back to the house, where I see what I think may be my favorite part, the patio. It's a covered space with a large fireplace, a dining table that looks to seat about half what the one inside seats with big, comfortable chairs around it, and a sitting area with colorful pillows. Each area is separated by carpet, and overhead hangs a huge Moroccan lamp.

"It's beautiful," I say, my eyes on everything, caught by it all, wanting to take it all in.

"The island isn't very big, so you won't get lost if you go for a walk, but you need to let someone know where you are at all times. The only part you're not allowed to go to is the east side."

"Why?"

"Because I said so."

"Which way is East? I have no sense of direction here."

He takes my hand, surprising me, and walks me to the opposite edge of the house and points. It's strange, but it's almost as though it's darker on that side of the island. Although I'm sure that's not true. And from above the trees, I see the gray stone roof of a building.

"What's there?" I ask.

"The family mausoleum."

"Oh." That's all he needed to say.

It's awkward for a moment, and I clear my throat.

"You said Lucinda Scafoni is your stepmother?"

"My mother died when I was two. Lucinda lived with us. She's my aunt, actually. My mother's sister. She married my father soon after my mother's death."

"Oh." That seems to be the only word I can speak today. "That's...weird."

"I guess." He actually smiles. Like a genuine smile.

"So your brothers are half-brothers?"

"Yes."

He's tight-lipped about his family, and I want more of the story, but there are more important things than his family history right now.

"Can I have contact with my family?"

He studies me.

"Just my Aunt Helena, maybe. She's very old. I'd like to call her."

"Tell her about our brutal ways?"

"She knows your ways. She was the Willow Girl seventy years ago."

He grows serious.

"I don't know how much longer she has." I don't say more because I already feel the backs of my eyes warming, as if the tear ducts are preparing to do their work.

"I'll think about it."

I almost want to argue, to push, but something tells me it'll be wiser to just give him some time. After all, he didn't say no.

I walk toward the pool, slip off a sandal, and dip my toe in the water. He follows me and takes a seat on one of the lounge chairs, legs wide like men tend to sit.

After slipping off both sandals, I walk to the edge of the tiled area and onto the grass. It's soft and cool beneath my feet as I make my way to what I think I saw from my room, a vegetable garden. It's much bigger than I realized. I pass two fig trees bursting with the fat, ripe fruit. I pick one, break off the stem, and watch creamy milk run down my palm. I eat it and pick another as I continue walking to where I hear the animals.

I see they have chickens and some lambs. One comes right up to the fence when he sees me, and I pet his curious head. I had a pet lamb when I was little. Well, it's not like she was given to me as a pet, I just made her that. Named her Honey. She was slaughtered soon after.

I still remember being made to sit at the table until I ate hours after my sisters had gone to bed. After that, I refused any meat.

When I head back toward the pool, I notice something up on a slight hill at the opposite end of the vegetable patch. It's the only ugly thing in sight, and it takes all I have to drag my eyes away. I only do when I hear him come up the path to meet me, and I know he's seen that I've seen it.

What had I thought, that he was joking? That it was a figure of speech?

I clear my throat. "Thanks for the tour. I'm going to go inside."

"But we're not finished."

I glance over his shoulder at the whipping post

again and take a step away, but he steps in my path and takes my arms.

His eyes grow dark, intense. I concentrate my attention on his neck. I can't hold his gaze.

"You didn't ask what that was," he says.

"Let me go."

"Ask."

"I don't need to."

"Ask anyway, Willow Girl."

I look up at him; I'd been avoiding his eyes. "Is this like Simon Says? You call me Willow Girl, and I have to do what you say?"

One side of his mouth curves upward. "You always have to do what I say."

"I'd almost forgotten."

"Ask me what it is, Willow Girl."

"I don't need to ask. I know."

He remains studying me so intimately, I can't look away.

"Say it."

"No."

"Say it, Helena."

"It's the post where you whip us Willow Girls."

His eyes have gone almost black, and I see his throat work when he swallows.

I shake my head, drop my gaze.

"This is archaic. This...reaping, the blocks, the whipping post," I say, and again, heat burns the backs of my eyes.

"It's tradition. It's the tradition of our families. You'll do it too, with your daughters, if you're the one to birth the quadruplets."

I shake my head. "The Willow Girl is never the one." The ring on my finger burns, and it's like it gives me strength. Like it's Aunt Helena giving me courage. "And if I were, I wouldn't give my daughters up, not without a fight."

"Your parents didn't fight."

"You think I don't know that."

"Would you have run? Is that why they bound you, shackled you? Would you have bit me? Is that why they gagged you?"

"I would have killed you if I could have."

He smiles, his eyes glow. "I like you, Willow Girl."

"I don't like you."

"You don't have to like me. You just have to obey me."

"I'm not afraid of you."

He laughs. "Yes, you are."

"No, you know what? You're right. Half right. I am afraid of what you can do to me. I mean, I've been here less than twenty-four hours, and I already wear the marks to show me exactly how the next three years will go."

"Do as I say, and you'll survive."

"By survive, you mean walk away after my time is up? What about after? Do you know the suicide rate of Willow Girls these days?" I feel my voice rising, wavering with emotion. "Do you?"

"Helena—"

"Why do you do it? Why take the girl? Now, I mean, in this day and age."

"I told you, tradition."

I shake my head, because that's not it. He's too modern for this. "There's something else. There has to be."

He cocks his head to the side. "Does it matter? I did take you. You're mine now. That's all you need to worry about."

We stand quietly, me watching him, him watching me.

He's right. It doesn't matter, not for me. Not anymore.

"Come with me."

He almost has to drag me up the path to the post, my legs growing heavier and heavier as we get nearer. When we finally stop in the clearing, I stare at my feet in the grass.

"Look up."

"I don't want to."

He moves behind me, holds me to him, and forces my head up by my chin. "Look up."

I do. And it looms over me, this stone post buried in the ground with shackles hanging from the top. I don't want to look too close because I see marks on it, areas that are worn smooth, and dark, human stains.

He walks me closer to it, and I'm powerless when he trails his fingers softly, like feathers, down my arms and captures my wrists. My heart races as he drags them upward, and the metal of the cuffs is cold when he closes them around my wrists.

"I didn't do anything," I say weakly.

"I have a question for you," he says, ignoring my comment, sliding the tips of his fingers back down my arms, to my sides, into the opening at the sides of the dress to cup my breasts. He kneads my nipples into points, and I swear I can feel his touch at my core.

I try to protest but my head drops back into the crook of his neck as he slips his right hand out and slides it lower, down to the front of the skirt of my dress, underneath it to my thigh, and up to my sex.

"Does it turn you on as much as it does me?" he asks, grinding his erection against my back while his fingers work my pussy.

I turn my face a little, so I can see him.

"It turns you on to have a woman bound to a whipping post?"

I suck in a breath when he pinches my clit.

"Not any woman. You."

"Me. A Willow Girl. A Willow Whipping girl."

He grips my hair and brings his mouth to my ear. "*My* Willow Whipping Girl."

I shudder.

"Now don't bite." He kisses me, and I don't bite, not this time. He slips his tongue inside my mouth. I'm so wet when he turns me, and the chains easily accommodate him.

Sebastian draws back and reaches behind my neck to untie the halter top.

I wonder if he planned this. If this is what he intended all along, giving me this particular dress. And I think the answer is yes when it falls to my feet and I'm naked and bound.

He pulls back to look at me, His fingers are working my pussy, and I'm so wet, I can hear myself.

"Come, Helena."

"No."

"Come."

"I don't want to."

I close my eyes, and he cups my ass with his other hand and squeezes. The pain makes me flinch, but then he kneads my clit, rubs it, smearing my own moisture all over it, and I suck in a loud breath and I know it's useless to fight him. I'm close, I'm so close. I open my eyes and see his smile and draw back or try to.

"I hate you," I say, the words forced as my knees buckle and I come. I come so hard it's running down my legs and I can hardly breathe because it feels so fucking good.

He leans in close to my ear, still working my clit,

still squeezing my ass. "Come on the post where your ancestors have been whipped raw. Where I'll whip you when your time comes."

I'm listening to him, my body shuddering with this forced pleasure. He doesn't let go of my pussy when it's finished, when the orgasm passes. Not yet. Instead, fingers smeared with his juices, he slides them backward, to my ass, and rubs and watches my face as he does.

"It's not all bad, is it, the whipping post. I'll teach you to come even when it hurts."

And as if to prove his point, he crouches down and cups my ass and squeezes hard, hurting the bruised flesh as he closes his mouth over my too sensitive clit and sucks. I come again, come on his tongue until I'm almost limp, my legs no longer able to hold me up.

He rises to his feet and grips my hair and kisses me hard. All I can taste is myself. Me on his tongue, his face. My scent clinging to him.

And then, a moment later, he stops, draws back. "What happened to you fighting me?" he asks, cocking his head to the side. "Where's the fight you promised?" His voice is low, deep, mocking.

"Let me down from here."

He reaches into his pocket and pulls out my pocket knife, opens it. He holds out his arm, and I watch him slice his skin, just below the crease of his elbow.

"What are you doing?" I ask.

"My notch."

He doesn't even flinch. Just closes the knife and looks at me. Any humor is gone from his eyes. He doesn't say a word as he pockets it and turns to walk away.

"Where are you going?" I yell after him, tugging at the restraints which seem to tighten as I struggle. "Sebastian!"

He stops, turns.

"I have a meeting," he says, making a point of checking his watch. "And as for what I'm doing, I'm being gentle with you, considering the caning you endured. Think of this as what you're owed for all the back talk, the bad behavior. I forget nothing, and I forgive nothing, not without punishment, Helena. Think about that as you spend a few hours here and thank your lucky stars this is all I'm doing."

"Come back! You can't leave me here like this. Come back, damn it!"

But he doesn't even look back. He just walks on, crosses the pool and disappears into the house.

8

HELENA

It's nightfall before I finally hear footsteps behind me, but when I turn, a new panic grips me when I see it's not Sebastian but Gregory. He's walking purposefully toward me, and I wonder when he got back to the island. If they're all back.

He's wearing a suit, the jacket still on, and when he reaches me, he stops, takes stock of my situation, and slips his jacket off his shoulders.

I don't know what to expect with him, but I'm not exactly in a position where I have much choice, so when he sets the jacket over my shoulders and wraps a strong arm around my middle before reaching up to undo the cuffs, all I can do is try to stand on my own legs, which aren't cooperating. My arms are worse, though. They're limp. I can't even manage to slap him away.

"Where's Sebastian?"

"He asked me to take you to your room. Stop struggling."

"I can walk."

"No, you can't. You can't even stand. How long did he have you out here?"

"All afternoon."

He makes a disapproving sound and carries me into the house and up to my room.

"Do you need to use the bathroom?"

I'm embarrassed, but I nod.

He walks me inside, and I try to squirm away. "I can do this part."

He ignores me and walks me to the toilet, sets me on it, then turns and walks out, closing the door behind him. I pee and with some effort, manage to clean myself. I stagger to the sink and am washing my hands when he opens the door and holds out an oversized T-shirt.

"What's that for?"

"I assumed you wouldn't want to sit around naked but if you'd rather—"

"No." Then, "I don't have clothes," I say stupidly.

He helps me to the chaise. My knees keep giving out, and I need his help.

"Can you lift your arms?" he asks.

I try but shake my head. He takes one arm at a time and dresses me like he would a child. It feels strange to have him do this. Almost intimate. And as soon as he slips the shirt over my head, I realize it's his. I can smell him on it.

"Why are you being nice to me?"

"I'm not. I'm just taking care of what's ours."

He sits down beside me and pulls the table closer. He picks up the glass of water and brings it to my lips.

I drink greedily, parched. When the glass is empty, he sets it down, picks up the spoon, and scoops up some soup. He brings it to my mouth, and I hesitate.

"What do you think? I'm going to poison you?"

I don't, but he doesn't wait for me to answer.

"You're a pain in the ass, you know that? I understand my brother. Just eat."

I open my mouth and drink the broth soup. It's good. So good.

"Can I have some wine?" I ask after finishing half the soup.

He puts the spoon down and pours me a glass of wine from the bottle. It's a rich, warming red, and it's exactly what I need.

"Thank you."

He nods. We don't talk while he spoon-feeds me the rest of the soup and the glass of wine.

"You know, you all act like I should just get over it already and be a good little whipping girl but put yourself in my place. How would you be if you were taken against your will and made a prisoner? If you were treated like I am here? I'm alone. Completely alone."

"Do you think you're the only person doing something against their will?" he asks, surprising me.

"I'm the only Willow I see here."

"Well, step back and look a little harder. You Willow's only see things from one perspective: yours. That's always been the problem."

"What do you mean?"

"I mean not all of us want to be here."

We both sit quietly for a minute until he stands.

"Do you need anything else?" he asks.

I shake my head. "No. I'll be fine."

"Good night, then." He walks to the door.

"Gregory."

He stops. "Yes?"

"Thank you."

"See, it's not so hard." With that, he walks out the door and I'm left alone in my room, the windows open to the clear night sky, alone with my bottle of wine.

Again trying to ignore the faint scent of him on the T-shirt, I use both hands to pour myself another glass, splashing some because even though the feeling is coming back, my arms are still weak.

I bring the glass to my mouth and drink a long swallow. I feel better for it and take it with me into the bathroom where I run a bath, pouring almost a full bottle of bubbles in.

After finally stripping off the T-shirt, I slide beneath the sudsy surface. I close my eyes as feeling slowly returns to my arms. I keep thinking about what Gregory said.

Who here is doing something against their will? Sebastian?

No. No fucking way.

I lay back, look up at the ceiling, follow the pattern of the molding. The scent of lavender makes me drowsy. I drink another sip of wine before setting the glass down on the edge of the tub and sliding both arms beneath the surface.

Sebastian is enjoying this. Enjoying my torment.

Gregory is wrong. He's not doing this against his will.

He may have felt sorry for me after Lucinda caned me, or, more likely, he felt usurped by her, that she was laying claim to a thing that's his. Taking his toy. That's more plausible to me.

I close my eyes for a while, listening to the only sound in the room, the occasional drip from the tap. I don't usually take baths. I don't take the time. But I have plenty of it now.

As I lie there, I think about how Gregory said what he said.

"You Willows only see things from one perspective: yours."

What's he trying to say? That Sebastian doesn't want to do what he's doing? That he's somehow forced to? Why?

But my thoughts are interrupted by Lucinda's voice in the distance, followed by a male voice and then her grating giggle.

I stand up, wrap a towel around myself, and tiptoe into the bedroom. The sound of an engine starting has me rushing to the window.

From here, I see them. Lucinda and Ethan are walking arm in arm. She's dressed in a long gown. Moonlight bounces off the gemstones around her neck. Ethan is in a suit or something like it. He helps her up the steps and onto the boat.

I recognize Gregory by his walk. He must be reading something on his phone, because I can see the screen's light from here. Sebastian follows last.

Earlier, I'd assumed Gregory was coming back from somewhere, not on his way to it when he came to get me. I am a little put off at being left behind. At the fact that Sebastian left me out there for so long, then sent his brother to collect me when he was here in the house all along. More than a little put off the more I think about it.

I duck back inside when Sebastian turns to glance up at my window and wait there, listening for the boat to leave. I dry off quickly, the feeling in my arms back now, and put Gregory's T-shirt back on then step out into the hallway and listen.

There's no sound, none at all, and I wonder if the staff has already gone home. I don't know what time it is.

The house is in semidarkness, lamps on here and there so it's not pitch-black. I go right and try the first door. It's an empty bedroom, the bed stripped, the windows closed. I leave it and go to the next, and I know it's Lucinda's because of the massive amounts of perfume that assault my senses when I stand in the doorway.

I step inside, leaving the door ajar. The first thing I do is look at the clock. It's a little after ten o'clock. I wonder where they were going dressed in their finest at this hour.

I walk around her room, noting the pile of dirty clothes on the floor. Probably left it for a maid to clean up after her. Her bed is made and on top of it are strewn three evening dresses, one still on its hanger with the tags attached. They're not my taste, but I can see they're expensive.

There's a desk along one wall. I go to it and pick up the envelopes stacked on top of it. Mail from the States and one from an Italian bank. They're sealed, so I put them back down.

I step back and survey the room and decide I'm wasting my time in here. If I'm alone in the house, I need to use my time wisely. I go back out into the hallway and try the last door on this side, which is locked. I pass my own room again and pause at the stairs to listen, then try the room adjacent to mine. I turn the handle and find it unlocked.

The instant I push it open, I know it's Sebastian's.

I go inside, and this time, I close the door behind me and lean against it. I just take a minute to breathe. To calm my frantic heartbeat. I'm too chicken to put on the lights, but the sky is clear, the moon is out and the bathroom light was left on, so I take in his room.

The king-size bed is central against the far wall with its headboard of carved wood that reaches practically to the ceiling. Pompous. Like he's a king.

The bed is made, the duvet a deep charcoal that matches his eyes. There's a worn leather armchair with a reading lamp over it and a shelf of books behind it, a large antique dresser, and two nightstands, each with a lamp on top.

There are three doors. The first leads to the bathroom with its light still on, the second is a walk-in closet.

Entering, I switch on the light in here and stop to inhale, recognizing the scent of his aftershave, not realizing I'd noted it, memorized it.

I run my hands along the suit jackets, of which he has a dozen or more. Next, slacks are hung that go with each one. Then the dress shirts. He's a neat freak. Everything is hung up or folded and color coordinated, the shoes polished and neatly in their cubbyholes. It makes me laugh, like I've found out a secret. Which is ridiculous. It's a closet.

On the island in the middle, I pull out the top drawer. He must have a hundred sets of cuff links, and at least eight watches.

I shake my head at the opulence. The abundance. How can some have so much while others starve?

Not that we Willows are starving, but there are people out there who don't have enough to eat, and this family has more than they will ever use up in their lifetimes.

I close the drawer and am about to step out of the closet when I notice something out of place on the floor. I bend to pick it up. It's my pocketknife. The one he stole from me. I grin, depress the button, and watch the blade open. At least he cleaned his blood off it.

Closing it, I slide it into the pocket on my borrowed T-shirt. He'll notice it's gone, I'm sure. He was having fun using it to carve out our various notches. Jerk.

I leave the light on and head back into the bedroom, going to the last door with a key in its lock. I turn and open it. I guess I shouldn't be surprised to see it leads to my room. Not that it matters which door he uses. He will enter at will and take what he wants at will and leave me hanging on a post for hours and then send his brother to get me at his fucking will.

From his windows, I see he has a better view than me. He can see more of the island. If I lean out, I can see the top of the mausoleum again. It makes me shudder. That part of the island, it just seems different.

I turn back in, go to his dresser, open the drawers, and rummage through them. I'm not looking for anything in particular. I just feel like I have some power right now. For the first time since I've been brought here. Like I'm in control.

How quickly it can be stripped from you.

The drawers in his nightstand are next. The one on the side of the bed closest to the door is empty, but when I go to close it, it sticks a little, so I try again, knocking the whole thing into the wall, making the lamp teeter.

I catch it before it falls and breathe a sigh of relief.

I walk around the bed to the other side, which must be the side he sleeps on, and am surprised to find the corner of a piece of paper sticking out of the drawer. I guess given the neatness of the room and his closet, I expected he'd be more careful putting things away.

I open the drawer and take out the sheet and notice the other items in the drawer—condoms and a tube of lubricant. I don't know why that surprises me. I'm sure he has women here. They're probably impressed when he brings them back to the island. *His* island. Probably can't wait to jump into his bed, in fact.

Which begs the question why would he want me? Or any unwilling Willow Girl? He's good-looking, he has money. Granted, he has a shitty family, but still. Why bother with me?

I shake my head and open the folded sheet of paper. It's a bank statement. My eyebrows go up at the figures I see.

I don't come from money. The Willows used to have money, but it's long gone. Even though we live on a huge piece of land, in what was once an opulent mansion but has lately been cheaply refurbished, even some parts of the house closed off. What we could do with money like this.

He must have been going through it with a fine-tooth comb, because there are markings along some of the lines, but it's the note scrawled on the side that catches my attention. I don't have time to investigate, though, when, out of the utter stillness of the night, the bedroom door crashes open and the lights go on and Sebastian is standing in the doorway, looking all huge and pissed off.

It takes me a full minute to process that I've been caught, and I stand there, dumbfounded as he looks at me, looks at the sheet in my hand, the open drawer.

"I saw you leave." It's all I can manage.

"I guess you saw wrong." He steps inside and closes the door, making a point of locking it and pocketing the key.

I swallow.

"What do you think you're doing in here?"

I look down at my hand, at the paper I'm still holding, and set it on the nightstand.

"Nothing. I couldn't sleep, so I thought I'd see if anyone was here." I'm so bad at lying.

"You thought you'd look in the drawers to make sure no one was hiding inside?" He gestures to the open one beside me.

"You said I was welcome—"

"In certain rooms of the house. My bedroom wasn't one of them, not to mention you rummaging through drawers." His eyes on me, he walks to the end of the bed across from me.

"In my defense, I didn't know this was your bedroom." I move to the other, and we're both watching each other.

"You have no defense," he says, shifting a little, me mirroring his move. "Whose shirt are you wearing?"

"Your brother's." I notice the slight narrowing of his eyes, the tensing of his jaw.

"Did he touch you?"

"To take me down from the whipping post you stuck me on, remember? And he was a perfect gentleman."

At that, he raises both eyebrows and seems on the verge of laughter. "I wouldn't bet on that, Helena."

I take advantage of his distraction. "I'll go back to my own room now if you're going to be that weird about things."

I take a step, trying to appear casual, like I don't know how much trouble I'm in, but he lunges toward me and I jump to the other side and scramble onto the bed to cross it to the door.

But it's a trick, because he anticipates my move and catches me easily, tosses me onto my back on the bed.

I let out a scream and roll onto my belly, get up on hands and knees to make my escape and about a second later, I'm yanked flat on my belly and he's got his full weight on me, his mouth at my ear. I feel his cock hardening.

"I don't want my brother's smell on you," he says, his voice low and deep, his breath at my cheek making me shudder.

I'm having a hard time breathing, but he gets up, kneels over me, and practically tears the T-shirt off me.

"What, are you worried he's marking your property?"

"Exactly." He turns me onto my back, keeps me safely tucked between his powerful thighs, and gives me a grin. He takes my wrists and spreads my arms out to the sides and leans in close. "Time to pay, Willow Girl."

He transfers my arms into one hand and reaches under the bed with the other, pulling out a pair of leather restraints. Squeezing my thighs between his, he binds my wrists and draws them over my head, clicking the cuffs into a ring attached to the headboard.

"What the hell is that?" I ask, trying to pull free.

He pulls his shirt over his head in one brisk move and fuck, he's so beautiful, all tanned olive skin and cut, hard muscle and all that ink. From the look on his face, he fucking knows it.

Sebastian leans down, inhales at my neck. "You stink of my brother." He licks my cheek. "I'll take care of that, though," he says as he starts licking me again like we're animals, like he's an animal licking his dinner.

I yank at the restraints even as my body remembers what he did earlier. Remembers how he made me feel. Even as it traitorously wants more.

"Get off me! Let me go, you fucking inbred prick!"

He stops at that, looks at me, and laughs outright.

"Not inbred, sweetheart, but I will give you prick."

I can see every one of his perfect white teeth as

his eyes take a quick sweep of me, pausing at my pussy, which is open to him given he's sitting between my legs. He runs two fingers over it before dragging his gaze back to mine.

"I like looking at you, Willow Girl," He wipes his fingers on my inner thigh. "And you like me looking."

"I don't, you sick inbred."

He leans down, pulls my pussy lips apart, and licks the length of me. I try to squeeze my legs closed, to shove him off, and pull on the cuffs, all to no avail.

"Told you already, not inbred," he says, straightening.

Giving me a wicked grin, he flips me onto my belly, the cuffs linked to allow it. He wraps his arms around my thighs and forces my ass up, my legs wide.

I crane my neck to look over my shoulder at him at eye level with my ass.

"Inbreeding would require blood relatives fucking and reproducing," he says, shifting his gaze to my ass.

"What are you doing?" What a stupid question. I know what he's doing. I just don't know what to do, how to react.

"I'm explaining how inbreeding works. Try to keep up."

Before I can reply, he buries his face in my pussy

and ass, and I suck in a loud breath at the sensation, at him, his tongue soft, a day's growth of beard rough as he licks my pussy, teases my clit, then drags his tongue up to my asshole and shifts his arms to tilt my hips so he has better access to me. A better view of me.

"Stop," I squeak. "You can't do that."

"I can do anything I want. Don't you know that yet?" He draws back, looks down at me, then dips his head down to taste me again, tastes all of me. "Your body is so responsive, Helena."

I bury my face in his pillow, and I can smell him on it. And fuck, what he's doing. His hands are on my ass, keeping me spread, fingers on me, tongue inside, and my body is like one giant nerve ending.

"Please," I arch my back. I'm pressing into him, and I'm so close when he pulls away and flips me onto my back.

"Not yet," he says. "Tonight, you're going to take my cock, come all over it while you keep telling me you don't want it, don't want me, Willow Girl."

He gets off the bed. His eyes are black, and he doesn't take them off me when he strips off his jeans and briefs and I see him for the first time.

He's huge and thick and ready.

"I don't want you!" I scream, trying to scramble away from him.

He climbs back on the bed and drags me back toward him by the ankle.

"Keep telling yourself that."

"I mean it." I squirm, but between him and the bonds at my wrists, I can only move inches.

"You're not going anywhere, Willow Girl," he says, again kneeling over me, his thighs on either side of my belly now. He leans back, eyes still on me as he scoops my pussy, lubricating his hand before taking his cock in it.

It takes all I have to drag my gaze up to his.

"You're not a virgin. Don't pretend to be scared, sweetheart."

I look down again, at his cock, at how it's growing even bigger in his hand. He reaches over my head and unhooks the cuffs from the headboard then unlocks each of them and throws them on the floor. He takes my wrists and spreads my arms wide again and lays on top of me so I can feel the wet tip of his cock on my belly and his face is so close, our eyes locked.

He kisses me, and it's deep and hard. I know it's how he'll fuck me, too—deep and hard and unforgiving. He shifts his grip from my wrists to my hands and interlaces our fingers together. I feel him start to slide inside me, and it hurts. He's too big, and I may as well be a virgin for all the sex I've had.

He turns my head to the side, kisses my cheek. "Relax." He draws out a little, pulling back to look at me. His eyes are shiny and completely black now.

He's watching me and moving inside me, and I know he's not even halfway in yet.

"You're too big. It hurts." When he releases my hands, I pull mine in and set them on his shoulders, try to push him off at least a little.

He touches my face, the side of my cheek, and I realize he's wiping away a tear. "You are so pretty when you cry, you know that?"

My belly quivers. He lifts up a little, and when he pushes one of my legs up, I look down and I see us, and we're connected. He's inside me, at least the tip of his cock is.

He touches my clit with his fingers and rubs, and I close my eyes and feel, feel his fingers on me, his cock stretching me, hard and soft and pain and pleasure.

But then he pulls out and turns me onto my belly. He's lifting my hips high, and when I try to rise, he pushes my head back down.

"Like this." He wraps one hand in my hair and squeezes my scalp. "Stay. Ass up, head down."

His other hand is between my legs, and it feels so good.

I lay my cheek down, and I watch him. He has one hand on my hip, the other underneath me, his gaze locked on my ass as he brings his cock to my pussy and pumps a little, penetrating me, taking a few inches more.

"You're wet and tight."

With that, he pulls his fingers from my clit and grips my hips. With his thumbs, he's pulling me wide open.

"So fucking tight." He meets my gaze and thrusts into me. The breath I'm taking catches in my throat, and I think I'm going to choke on it.

I grip the sheets, groan into them, and when I try to bring my head up, he again fists a handful of hair and shoves it back down.

Sebastian thrusts again, then draws out. He's hovering at the entrance of my sex.

He brings his thumb to my asshole, and the fingers of his other hand are at my clit again. He fucks me, really fucks me, and he's not gentle and it hurts and it feels so fucking good.

I can't tell what's what. All I feel is him, him all around me, his scent on the pillow my face is buried in, him behind me, his fingers on me, inside me, his cock tearing me in two, tearing me apart.

And then, when I think I'll rip apart, when I think I can't take any more, I come. I fucking come, and the sound I make is strange, foreign and the pain and the pleasure are mixed up, confused. I can't think anymore, not when I feel him throb, not when I hear him grunt, call out, not when he slams into me one last time, and not when I feel him empty inside me, using me up, filling me up, taking all of me, owning me.

I fall onto the bed when he releases me. The

room smells of sex. I feel cum slide out when he gets up and goes into the bathroom. I hear the water go on. I lie there, trying to make sense of this, of what just happened.

He comes back a few minutes later and climbs back onto the bed, rolls me onto my back, and cleans me. He's so gentle that I want to cry. It makes no sense, but I can't help it. I just lie there, and I cry. I fucking sob, and I don't understand why.

I hate him.

This is easy.

Simple.

Fucking simple.

I'm a Willow, and he's a Scafoni, and I hate him. And that's all.

But I didn't fight him. I didn't even try. He untied me, and I didn't even try.

I came instead.

My eyes are closed, but I feel him watching me.

Maybe he likes it. He thinks I'm pretty when I cry.

I don't think he meant sobbing, though. Sobbing is all choked breath and snot, and this is that and I don't fucking understand what's happening to me.

He switches out the lights from somewhere beside the bed and pulls my back into him.

I shake my head no, and push off, press the heels of my hands into my eyes.

"Let me go. I want to go to my room."

"Shh. Lie down now, Helena."

"Willow Girl. I'm the Willow Girl."

He shouldn't call me by name.

"Shut the fuck up and go to sleep." He forces me down, holds me to him, his arm like a vice around me.

"My aunt...My Aunt Helena, she said there's a reason I was chosen. Because I shouldn't have been. I had the blood on my sheath to mark me."

He's quiet, listening. I can hear him breathing behind me, feel his heart beating against my shoulder. Feel his warmth, his strength, envelop me.

"She thinks I'll be the one to end this."

The crying starts again, but this time, it's this choked sound, and I have to force down the lump in my throat to keep going.

"She thinks I'm strong, like her." I touch my ring with my thumb. "But she doesn't know that when I found out, when my mother told us what would happen to us, what we'd have to do, she doesn't know what I did."

"What did you do?"

"We were sixteen. I don't think any of us even ate the birthday cake after that. It's kind of a spoiler, huh?" I almost laugh but this isn't funny.

"What did you do, Helena?"

"I went out to the barn, and I fucked the boy who worked for us. I fucked him because I didn't want to be the Willow Girl."

It's quiet for a long minute.

"Just go to sleep, Helena. It doesn't matter anymore."

"My mom caught us. The boy and his father both lost their jobs. I just got a belting. The only time my father laid a hand on me, and it was my mother who demanded it. I guess she knew why I did it. Knew she'd lose one of her golden daughters because of me."

I roll onto my back, then turn to him. His eyes are open, but I can't tell what he's thinking.

"I guess we have that in common," I say.

"What?"

"My mom and your stepmom. They're more violent than our dads. At least mine, I guess."

"Go to sleep, Helena. You can join the shitty childhood club tomorrow. Just go to sleep now."

"I couldn't walk for three days after that, and it was all for nothing, wasn't it?"

It's quiet for a long time. I think I doze a little too, but every time I open my eyes, he's there, still awake, still keeping watch over me.

"I don't think you're weak, Helena," he says finally. "Scared isn't the same as weak. Forget the past. It doesn't matter anymore."

"No, it doesn't. I'm still here, and I'm still scared."

SEBASTIAN

Forget the past.

That's the thing about being a Willow or a Scafoni. You can't ever forget the past. It doesn't let you. And neither does the present.

I know about her aunt, the woman she's named after. The other Willow with black hair and a silver streak through it. The Willow Girl who almost beat her Scafoni master. Who almost broke him. Who almost broke the family apart.

But that wasn't the end of the story.

Helena should know better her history.

And the thing about ending this, there's no such thing. Not for her. Not for me. And not for future generations of Willow daughters or Scafoni sons.

I look over at her standing beside me as I dock the boat. It's been three days since the night I caught her in my room, and I can't seem to stop looking at her.

We've just reached Venice proper, and her eyes are as wide as saucers as she takes it all in. It's summertime, which means one part of the floating city will be overrun with tourists.

It's amazing to me that people will travel hundreds of miles over hours and days and never leave one tiny part of Venice with all its vendors selling worthless trinkets, the noise and smell of a thousand people taking pictures of the filthy pigeons in the square, of the gondola with the singing gondolier. Fucking tourist traps. What they're seeing isn't Venice—at least, not my Venice.

"I thought there would be more people," Helena says when we disembark.

"There are. On the other side. This is the Cannaregio district. It's the better side, without the throngs of tourists. I'm not much of a people person."

She stops, turns to me. "That's a shocker."

"Don't be a smart-ass. Come here." She's already walking off, distracted.

It's been one week since she's been on the island with us, and I should have brought her here sooner. Should have done it on the day she arrived.

"I want to see the church," she calls over her shoulder.

"We can see it after."

"It's just a few minutes. I want to light a candle." And she goes off ahead of me, following the two nuns toward the small wooden door at the side of the old church.

"Do you ever listen?" I ask, taking her by the arm when I catch up with her. I walk her around the corner and to the steps of the entrance. "Here."

"Oh."

She looks up at it. It is a beautiful church. Most of Italy's churches are, and Venice's especially, although I'm partial, since this is home. Religion is an important part of Italian culture—at least for most people.

"Thanks," she says.

I nod, and we walk in, my hand at her lower back, her heels clicking on the stone steps. The clothes I ordered for her had come, and today she's wearing a gray skirt and a white, short-sleeved blouse with dark pumps. When I told her what we were doing, she'd chosen the most somber outfit she could find.

The soft scent of incense hovers outside the church. We approach the doors and I pull one open only to have that incense rush my senses. We walk inside, and she stops. Me too.

There's a stillness here, something rare and unique to churches. Even if there's a mass in session and a hundred faithful in the pews and an organ blaring out a Gothic hymn, underneath it is stillness.

It's here now, something I not only hear but feel deep in my bones, right to my marrow.

I know the exact day I stopped believing in God. It wasn't when my mother died but the day I learned that the church turned its back on her. She who spent more time on her knees in prayer than anyone should.

I was a toddler when she died. Too young to experience that much loss, that much sadness. At least that's what people thought. But I saw everything and heard everything and remembered it all.

It wasn't until years later that I realized why everyone was so angry at her. I didn't understand why my father suddenly turned his back on the church. I was seven when I finally did, and that was when I turned my back too. Finally understanding my father's curse against our priest for not burying her. For refusing to even hold mass for her soul.

But Catholics are strange when it comes to suicide.

"I'll wait outside," I say, my voice hoarse.

Helena is surprised, but I turn and go, and I don't explain myself.

I don't want to be in there. I want to scrub the stink of incense from my clothes, my hair.

My mother used to say it's the smell Jesus loves, that's why it's always burning. This made perfect sense to me when I was little. Now, it turns my stomach, excavating memories better left buried.

Fifteen minutes later, I watch her push open the heavy door and step outside. She smiles when she spots me, which I don't expect. But maybe she doesn't either because she schools her features into a frown a few moments later.

I take her arm. "You're prettier when you smile."

"I'm not really going for pretty."

I shrug a shoulder.

"I've always wanted to visit Venice, but not like this. Not for this," she says.

"It won't take long. My attorney's offices are just a few blocks away, and then, if you're good, I'll take you to lunch afterward."

"Wow, really?" she asks, hopping in front of me, mimicking an excited child. "Will you buy me a Popsicle too if I'm a good little girl? Huh? Will you?" She gives a shake of her head and falls back in line beside me. "Prick," she mutters under her breath.

I take her arm, tug her close. "No, no Popsicle for you. I was planning on giving you something else to suck on, but if you're not careful, you'll get it up your ass instead."

She glances up at me from the corner of her eye, and I can almost see the names she's calling me on the inside. Which is fine, as long as I don't have to hear them.

"That time on the post didn't do much for your attitude, did it?" I ask as we turn a corner and are, thankfully, out of the sun. It's warmer here than on the island. Must be all the bricks. Just sucks up the heat.

"My attitude is just fine. I haven't called you an inbred since you so kindly educated me on the specifics, have I?"

"You're a quick study when you're getting your pussy eaten out."

"Jesus. Why are you so crude?"

I glance at her. "Some women find dirty talk hot."

"I don't know. I think it depends how good the dirty talker is."

"Touché." I stop. "Hand me the switchblade you took from my room. That's a notch for you."

From the look on her face, she didn't think I'd notice.

That, or she thinks I'm stupid.

"You stole it from me first. I just took back what was mine to begin with."

"Just take care with it. I don't want you hurting yourself, Willow Girl."

"You prefer to do all the hurting, is that it?"

"Careful there." I wrap my hand around the back of her slender neck and give a little squeeze. "Part of the deal is I return you in one piece."

It's her who stops now just as we get to the entrance of the building. "Physically, at least, right? Doesn't matter about the scars inside. Just all fingers and toes accounted for."

I feel one eye narrow. "Something like that."

She always takes it just a hair too far, but I get the feeling part of that is her fighting herself because as far as sex goes, she comes at least twice a day since the night I caught her in my room. And she's always game, no matter how much she tries to tell herself and me she's not.

"Let's go up. Get this done."

We walk into the ancient building that houses our attorneys. The building itself is part of Scafoni family holdings. It's been beautifully restored. Upon entering, I think about how much I pay our attorneys to keep our secrets.

Helena is awed. I can see it on her face. She's taking everything in, from the pattern of the marble on the floor to the paintings and tapestries hanging on the walls. I understand. It looks more like a palace than an office.

The receptionist stands to greet us, coming around the desk, almost bowing to me. I guess she knows who pays for her designer suit and shoes.

When I introduce her to Helena in English, she apologizes for speaking Italian and continues in English, telling us that Mr. Gallo will be with us shortly and asking if we'd like something to drink.

"Cappuccino please," Helena says.

"An espresso for me." She nods and walks through the door that leads to the small kitchen to work on our coffees.

"This building is amazing." Helena turns a circle, eyes up, down, every which direction.

"Thank you. We had it reconstructed to look like it did in its early days, and it was a much bigger job than I realized. There was quite some water damage—it renders the first floor almost completely unusable—but the rest of the building is in perfect condition."

"You own the building?"

I put my finger to her chin to close her mouth.

She clears her throat. "I just don't even understand how much money that is."

"It's important to preserve the architecture of the city. This isn't only my family's inheritance. And by that, I mean culturally. The Scafoni family has an obligation to the people of Venice. I take that very seriously."

"Do you own more buildings here? Is that where Scafoni money comes from?"

"A few and some." I lead her around.

"Some?"

"Some of our wealth is through real estate. Some...outside of real estate."

She looks at me suspiciously. "Legal?"

I give her a wide grin.

"Are you like a local mafia family or something?" I think she means it as a joke.

"This way," I say, not answering.

She seems to understand I won't be explaining further.

"This building dates back to the fourteenth century, and it was home to the Michiel family for a time."

"I don't know who that is."

"Venetian nobility."

"Oh. Are you Venetian nobility too? That's a stupid question."

"It's not stupid."

"I don't know anything about this. We don't have this in America."

He smiles. "No, we're not nobility. We're just smart businessmen."

She studies me, and I wonder what she's thinking, what she wants to say. She's clever enough to know that you have to be better than smart to have collected our sort of wealth and power, and that doesn't always come without darker dealings.

"Why don't you have an accent when you speak English?" she asks.

"Because I was educated in boarding school in Massachusetts. I only spent summers in Italy."

"Your brothers too?"

"Yes."

Before she can ask another question, we're interrupted. "Sebastian, I'm so sorry to keep you waiting."

I turn to find Joseph Gallo coming down the stairs. He's dressed impeccably, as usual. I've been working with him since I took over the family after my father died and have known him for most of my life.

I shake his hand, patting his shoulder. "Twice in one week."

Joseph Gallo handles the Willow transactions. He's the one I came to see to discuss payments a few days ago.

"A fortunate week," he says elegantly.

He turns to Helena and takes her in, then holds out his hand. "Miss Willow, I presume." He doesn't quite shake her hand but holds one of hers inside both of his and turns to me. "Each generation is more beautiful than the last."

I catch Helena's glance. Joseph Gallo handled the details with Libby Willow too.

"Let's go upstairs. Everything is ready. Should only take a few minutes."

Her mood soured, Helena walks up the stairs only because of the pressure of my hand at her back. She isn't even looking around anymore but is instead lost in her own thoughts as we enter Joseph's office.

"Sit down, please," he says, gesturing to two large, comfortable chairs before his antique desk.

The receptionist approaches with a tray of coffee for each of us and places a small plate of cookies on the table between our chairs.

Helena leaves hers untouched. I notice how her hands curl around the arms of the chair as she watches Joseph, who casually sips his espresso as he opens the large leather-bound tome before him.

Joseph sets his cup down and looks up at us, smiling as if any of this is normal.

"I don't know how much Sebastian has explained to you, but I'll just go through the legalities before you sign."

"What legalities? There aren't any. Don't pretend like this is just a normal, everyday transaction."

He isn't ruffled. "We like to keep a recording for the sake of history."

She raises her head to peek at the book on the desk, and Joseph turns to me.

I nod my head, and he turns the heavy book and sets it at the edge of the desk. She leans forward and looks at the still empty pages where her name is typewritten beneath one of the two lines there. Mine is beneath the other. The paper is specially made for us with our family crest embossed on it. Each page contains a rectangular frame sized for an 8x10 photo.

She touches it, traces one part of it, then turns the heavy sheet backward and stops.

Her Aunt Libby is staring back at her. Two photographs. One when she arrived on property, and one on the day before her release.

Beneath each image is a date and a signature, one belonging to her, the other to my father. The oldest son is the one responsible for the girl over the three years.

Helena stands to get a better look. She touches the photograph, then turns the page backward again, to the ones containing the two photographs her great-aunt.

"There aren't many of you born with dark hair," Joseph says. "Or at least not the chosen girls."

She looks up at him with hate in her eyes.

"I guess the Scafoni men have a preference for blondes, but I don't think chosen is the right word. This isn't a privilege. It's a condemnation."

"Helena," I warn.

She ignores me and returns her attention to her aunt's image.

I don't need to look to see what she sees. I've memorized this tome. And I know that as she scrolls through the pages of the Willow Girls who came before her, her namesake will be the only photograph where in the second image, the girl still has life in her eyes. Is still wearing a smile.

In the case of her aunt, the smile appears almost demented. Maybe she'd gone insane by the end.

Joseph begins explaining what will happen today. She's still looking through the book though, back to when photographs were black-and-white, back when instead of photographs, hand-drawn sketches fill the pages. She then turns through the rest of it, flipping through all the empty pages, the destinies of the future Willow Girls, until she has enough and slams the book closed.

"Let's get this done, then. Where do you want me?" Her hands are fisted.

I rise to my feet.

She's looking around the room like she's searching for a spot.

"This is your second warning," I say, squeezing her elbow.

She turns to me, fire burning in her eyes. "I don't care."

Joseph rises, clears his throat. "This way," he says, not an ounce of formal elegance lost as he opens a door to a smaller room off his office.

Helena doesn't move at first, doesn't move until I nudge her. When we pass Joseph into the room, he gives me a knowing smile.

"There's always a bit of this at the first photograph," he says, emphasis on the word *first*.

She turns to him, and I wrap my hand around her arm because she's going to leap at him.

Joseph holds up a hand. "She's new, Sebastian. Hasn't yet learned. I promise it will be very different very soon. As soon as you get a handle on her."

"A handle on me?" Helena snorts. "Like a leash? How do you know, anyway, that it'll be different?" she asks. "Do you visit the island? See what they do? Join in?" She tries to pull free, but I squeeze. "You're all sadists, you know that?"

He only smiles.

"Give us a few minutes, please, Joseph."

"Of course." He leaves the room, closes the door behind him.

I release her as soon as he's gone and unbuckle my belt. "Against the wall. Lift your skirt." I pull my belt loose of the loops and watch her jump at the whooshing sound of it.

"Go to hell!"

I stalk over to her, covering the space in just three steps. Frantically looking around, she picks up the only thing in the room besides the camera set on its tripod, which is a wooden stool.

"I'm warning you, Sebastian!"

I almost chuckle, grab a leg of the stool and tug, pulling her off balance, relieving her of it. She stumbles as the stool goes clattering to the ground, laying on its side. She takes a step backward, presses her back against the wall. I double the belt in my hand, squeeze the buckle of it in my palm, feel the metal dig into my skin, breaking it.

"Turn around and lift your skirt."

"Like I said, go to hell."

"Oh, Helena. You are fun. Turn."

"You'll have to make me."

"With pleasure."

I spin her around and wrap one hand around the back of her neck and, without a second thought, I raise my right arm and bring the belt down on the backs of her calves.

She cries out, tries to cover herself.

I raise the belt again and this time, bring it down on the crease of her knees, the sound of leather on flesh making my dick hard.

Her cry is louder this time, and I quickly follow it up with a third stroke.

"Ready to lift your skirt?"

"I hate you. I hate you so much!"

I lean in close, my mouth to her ear. "I don't care." I strap behind her knees once more, and they buckle.

"Your ass, Helena. Now. Or you won't be walking for the next few days."

She's crying, and she moves slowly, but finally her trembling hands raise her skirt up to her waist.

"Bare."

With one hand, she pushes her panties off her hips, and they drop to her ankles. Keeping one arm at her back to keep her skirt lifted, she sets the other into the wall and presses her face into it. Both hands are fisted.

"Now stand still," I tell her, an edge to my voice. "This is going to hurt."

I release her neck and step back to rain ten strokes on her sweet little ass, watching each thick stripe rise and redden, covering the whole of her ass and the tops of her thighs before I stop.

The room is quiet but for her ragged breath.

"Do you need more?"

She shakes her head no.

"You sure?"

She nods.

"Good." I drop the belt to the floor, then right the stool and go to her, turn her to face me.

Her breathing is ragged, her eyes puffy and wet with tears.

"You fight me, Willow Girl, and you'll lose. Every single time."

"I will never stop fighting you, Sebastian. Not ever. Whatever you do to me, I will never stop. I swear it."

I slide one hand between her legs and rub her pussy, her swollen clit, and bring my mouth to hers.

"I'll hold you to that," I say.

Our eyes locked, she opens her mouth against mine and rises on tiptoe. I can feel her breath on me, shallow and hot. I undo my pants, shove them and my briefs just far enough to free my dick, and lift her up only to impale her on my cock, watching the expression on her pretty, tearstained face change, pulling out to thrust in again, then again.

I kiss her mouth, feel her little teeth biting down on my lip as I cup her ass and knead it.

"I hate you," she whispers, clinging to me as her pussy tightens around my cock.

"But your body doesn't." I bite her back, liking the taste of the iron of her blood. "Your cunt loves my cock, Willow Girl. It's dripping for me."

She digs her nails into my shoulders and buries

her face in my neck to muffle her cry when she comes, when her cunt pulses around me, wet and hot and tight, milking my cock, taking my seed inside her as she cleaves onto me, sagging into me, breathless, empty.

I pull out and set her on her feet.

Her knees wobble, and she has to hold on to me so as not to fall down.

I pick up her panties, help her step into them, and pull them up.

"I need to use a bathroom," she says. "Clean up."

I shake my head. "After. I want you to feel my cum inside you. Feel me dripping out of you."

I wipe the last of the tears off her face, comb her hair with my fingers. I cup the back of her head and make her look at me when she pushes against me, taking in her sad eyes, the defeat inside them.

"Why do you do this?" she asks.

"It doesn't have to be hard." I barely whisper it. I know we're not unobserved. "You make it hard."

A perfect teardrop falls from her eye. I capture it under my thumb, smear it across her cheek.

When she's like this, soft and a little beaten, I feel like I can get lost inside the endless night sky of her eyes, and I don't want to look away.

She's a Willow Girl. I'm a Scafoni son. Firstborn, almost. We're both condemned. But if I'm not careful, it can be worse, so much worse for the both of us.

I pull back and kiss her once more on the mouth. Our eyes are open. It's not an erotic kiss. I don't pry her lips open to slide my tongue inside. It's just a kiss, and at the same it's the most intimate kiss.

When I release her, she staggers to the stool a few feet away and sits on it like she can't stand anymore. I wonder what she thinks when she looks at me. What she feels.

She must hate me. She must curse me.

I pick up my belt to weave it through the belt loops and open the door. Joseph is at his desk. He watches me buckle the belt.

He heard everything, I know, and he's not my friend, I know that too. There are no friendships when this much money is in play.

He smiles and gets up from his desk to make his way into the room again. I know the camera in the ceiling recorded everything. I know he'll watch right after we're gone. I know he'll get hard at Helena's cries. Jerk off to her whipping. Our fucking.

The room smells of sex. Of us.

Joseph glances at Helena, and her cheeks burn. She, too, knows he heard every damn thing.

"Are we ready, then, Miss Willow?"

I put my hand around the back of her neck. "I think she's ready now, aren't you, Helena?"

She won't look at us, but I can see from her profile that she's biting her lip to stop from speaking or maybe crying.

"All right. If you'll kneel on the stool, please," Joseph says.

She turns to me. "Kneel?"

I hold out a hand to help her. "Kneel," I say.

She swallows but rises and doesn't take my hand as she kneels on the wooden stool and turns to the camera. Just as he snaps the photograph, she gives him the finger.

I can't help the smile that creeps along my lips.

Joseph, however, is not amused. His ears go red, and it may be the first time I've seen him ruffled.

"We'll need to take another."

But it's an old-fashioned camera. Not a digital one.

"No need, Joseph," I say, looking at my pretty, defiant Willow Girl. "That'll do just fine."

10

HELENA

We both signed the book in the space where my photo will be forever preserved as this generation's Willow Girl. We're now sitting at a table for two waiting for our lunch to arrive.

Our eyes are locked, but the difference in our expressions is night and day. I'm glaring, and he looks like he's smiling, calm as can be, like this is normal.

"What's your problem?" I ask finally, shifting in my seat, his cum sticky in my underwear.

"No problem. Just enjoying my day with my Willow Girl."

"You know he heard everything."

He nods. "He's probably jerking off to the video as we speak."

"Video?"

Sebastian shrugs a shoulder.

A waiter comes with a bottle of wine, pours for both of us, and sets the bottle in a bucket of ice before leaving.

"Don't worry. You shouldn't have to see him again for three more years." He picks up his glass. "Cheers."

I fold my arms across my chest. I don't pick up my glass.

"How did it start? Taking a Willow Girl?"

"You don't know your history?"

"No, I don't. Why don't you educate me, like you so graciously did on the meaning of inbred." Prick, I add internally.

"Happy to oblige." He takes another sip of his wine. "The Willows were a prominent family—at least in the Midwest—way back when. The Scafoni were immigrants to America, but wealthy ones. We needed status, and you needed money, and so a marriage was arranged.

"There was a difference then, and that was that the Willows only had sons and the Scafonis only daughters, and so a Willow boy, Marius Willow, married a Scafoni girl, Anabelle Scafoni, for her fortune. There was no love between them. It was a business transaction, one arranged by Anabelle's father and Marius Willow. He was more than twice her age and a brute, according to history."

"According to your history," I interrupt.

He ignores me.

"She didn't survive long in his hands. Not a full year, even. In fact, only a handful of Scafoni survived that marriage. Marius Willow made sure of that, having no pity, killing off as many as he could, starting with Anabelle's father. Although I guess he did have some pity. He didn't kill Anabelle or her mother but cast them out, left them for dead, after securing Anabelle's fortune. If he'd killed her, none of this would be happening."

"Why?" I'm engrossed.

"There was one thing he didn't know when he sent her out of his house. Anabelle was pregnant."

"Pregnant?"

He nods. "Anabelle's mother, who was a midwife, cared for her, and delivered the baby in secret. This was a rare male birth for the Scafoni family. Just two months after the baby's birth, Anabelle died. She was too broken by her grief. It's a wonder the baby didn't die with her."

"What happened to the baby?"

"After burying her daughter, Anabelle's mother, took the child and fled back to Italy, but not before laying a curse on the Willow family, one that would weaken their line. From that point, the Willow family only had girls and the Scafoni family only boys."

"A curse? You can't believe in that."

His expression and his non-comment give me

pause. I don't expect Sebastian Scafoni of all people to be superstitious.

"Anabelle's son, Giuseppe, was raised to hate the Willow family, and when he came of age, he vowed vengeance for his mother and set upon rebuilding our fortune, passing down his hate from generation to generation until we were ready to return to America. To avenge Anabelle."

"But how? Even back then, what you're doing couldn't have been legal. I mean, it's kidnapping."

"You're naive, Helena."

"No, I'm—"

"If you have enough money, you can do anything you want. Have anything you want. Money is power. Money makes us kings. Gods even."

I shake my head. "What do you hold over the Willows that they don't put a stop to it?"

"I just told you."

"You told me money makes you a god."

"Money got me you."

"I don't understand."

"It's actually much simpler than you think. You sure you want to hear it?"

"Yes."

"It may change your view of your family."

"It won't."

"The Willow property, have you ever seen the deed?"

I shake my head.

"I'm not surprised. Our name is on it. The Scafoni family owns the estate."

I snort at that. "You want me to believe you own our house?"

"And the land it's built on."

"I don't believe you. The house has been in our family forever."

"Not really. Not in almost two hundred years."

"What are you saying? You...buy the Willow Girls?"

He shrugs a shoulder. "I think of it as more of a lease."

"What are you talking about? My parents wouldn't allow—"

He leans in close. "Your parents were eager, Helena."

His words hit me like a punch to the gut. I don't know if that's what he intended, because he picks up his wine, gives a shake of his head, and swallows a large mouthful.

The waiter appears with our lunch, but I've lost the little appetite I had.

Without a word, Sebastian picks up his knife and fork and cleans his fish, then takes a bite. "It's good. You should eat."

He puts another forkful into his mouth. I don't move, I don't touch my utensils.

I look up from my plate of pasta with red sauce,

notice the anchovies lying on top. Why do people think vegetarians eat fish?

"I don't believe you," I say.

"I made the first payment the day you got to the island. It was on the statement you were holding when you were snooping in my room."

"You're lying."

"Why would I lie? Why would I need to?"

"You want to turn me against my family."

"What purpose would that serve?"

He's right.

"I mean, think about it, a sacrifice of one for the survival of the family. It's a deal I wouldn't make, but the Willows never did have much integrity. Even family doesn't mean anything to them. They sell off their daughters like they do a prize pig."

I meet his eyes, and he's dead serious. He's not making fun of me or trying to injure me.

"I can prove it to you if you want. I'll show you all the bank statements. All the payments made to the Willows for the sacrifice of one daughter with every generation."

I pick up my glass then, take a long swallow. My hand is trembling when I set it down.

"And you're okay with it? With taking me? Knowing I don't want to be here. Will you be okay to hand me to your brothers?"

At that, he pauses, exhales, takes a moment to look across the room then back at me. "What I want and what I have to do are not always one and the same, Helena."

"So you don't want this?"

"I didn't say that."

"Could you have said no?"

"What do you think would have happened if I did? Do you think Lucinda or Ethan or even Gregory would have let it go?"

"What do you mean?

His face darkens. He sets his utensils down and leans in.

"I mean if I chose not to participate, Ethan would have happily taken my place. But I guess that would have been good news for you. He'd have chosen one of your sisters."

He sits back, picks up his fork and knife again.

"You talk about a way out, but there isn't one, Helena."

He reaches across the table and forks through my pasta, shakes his head. I just watch, slow to process his words, as he calls the waiter over. I know he's sending my plate back, explaining about the fish.

The waiter apologizes, and I nod my head, but I'm not really listening. He's back a few minutes later with a fresh plate minus the fish.

But it's a waste of food.

I can't eat a bite.

I'm on my fourth glass of vodka as I stare, bleary-eyed, at the papers before me. I guess I can't understand why he told me. What's the point? To hurt me? To make sure I know I am fully alone? Because I already knew that. I've known that for a long time.

As promised, Sebastian delivered the statement I'd found while snooping to my bedroom the next night along with records of past payments, almost two hundred years-worth of them. He also showed me a copy of the deed.

It's true. We live on Scafoni land.

I wonder if my Aunt Helena knows. If my sisters know, now that I'm gone, and it's settled, at least for the time being. Until they have their daughters, and the Scafoni have their sons.

There's one discrepancy I don't understand, though. The payments are made three times, once every year. I assume it's done when the Willow Girl is passed from brother to brother.

There used to be four payments, but for the last several reapings, only three have been made and there are only the three brothers.

But that thought is pushed aside by the others. Mainly, my parents' betrayal of me. But also the other thing. About having no choice.

I have a hard time believing Sebastian doesn't

want this, not now that he has it, even if he didn't think he wanted it at first. And I can't think about what will happen in a year's time.

Sebastian is cruel, merciless when he punishes me, but there's something else too. A protectiveness, a possessiveness almost. I'm his. And in a way, as long as I'm his, I'm safe.

No.

I shove the papers off me and get to my feet so quickly, that between the blood rushing and the vodka, I have to hold on to the wall so as not to fall over.

I'm not safe.

And I can't be fool enough to let myself think I am, not for a second.

I stand taller. I steel my spine and say it out loud. "I am not safe. Not with him. Not with any of them."

Does he think that by telling me, by isolating me mentally and emotionally as well as physically, that I'll be a better Willow Girl. A more obedient one?

I go to the window, wrap my sweater around myself because tonight is cooler than it has been, and I think about them, about my family and how they betrayed me. How they've been betraying their daughters for generations. And for what? Money. For fucking money.

"Willows never did have much integrity. Even family doesn't mean anything to them. They sell off their daughters like they do a prize pig."

His words slam into me but before they can break me, I stalk to the nightstand and open the drawer and take out my pocketknife. I don't know why he didn't take it from me. It's not an oversight. Sebastian doesn't overlook anything.

Three million dollars. If I survive the three years. That's the sum of it. Of my worth.

I know our house is important. I know the land is important. But isn't a daughter more important?

I gather up the papers, not caring that I'm crushing them. I want to rip them to shreds, even if they are copies.

I walk out of my room. I don't even close the door behind me.

He's downstairs, in his study. I know because he told me he'd come up for me when he was finished with his work. Needs his nightly fuck, I guess.

Two Willow Girls have died while serving their time, and when my Aunt Helena was the Willow Girl, only two payments were made. Did she run away? Did she manage to stay away for a time? Because there was a clause that should the girl not be available to the Scafoni sons, the Willow family would be penalized, and that penalty would be paid in the form of a forfeiting of funds, or worse.

The words *an eye for an eye* stand out.

They make me shudder.

I look down at my ring.

Bone for bone?

My mother, when she told us what would happen to us, she didn't quite tell it like this. Never mentioned money, just a debt, and warned us that whoever was chosen would have to serve the full three years. She told us we'd not be welcome home because the vengeance the Scafoni would take would be catastrophic to the rest of the family.

The house is dark but for the light under the study door. It's past one in the morning, but Sebastian isn't alone in there. I hear two male voices.

I don't bother to knock but push the door open. I guess I push too hard because it slams against the doorstop and vibrates. Sebastian looks up from behind his desk, momentarily surprised. Only momentarily.

I turn from him to the chair across the desk to find Gregory there.

"Helena," Sebastian says, pushing back from his desk and folding his arms across his chest. "How can I help you?"

Ignoring Gregory, I slam the papers down in front of him.

"Why did you tell me? What's the point?"

He cocks his head to the side, studies me. "Are you drunk?"

My hands fist so hard that I feel my fingernails digging into my palms. "Why?"

I hear a chuckle.

I turn to Gregory, who stands and looks at me.

He doesn't bother to school his features into something more serious.

He shifts his gaze to Sebastian.

"I'll say good night, brother. We'll pick up tomorrow."

"Good night," Sebastian says. I don't think his eyes ever leave mine.

Gregory closes the door behind him. Sebastian gets up and comes to me.

"It's rude to barge into someone's office like that, Helena."

"I don't much care about rude."

"No, you don't. How much did you drink?"

"Not enough. Why? Why did you tell me?"

"You asked, remember? And I warned you that you may not like what you hear."

"Is it to isolate me even more? Make sure I know I can't go home?"

"Watch your tone, Helena."

"Don't you mean Willow Girl? Watch your tone, Willow Girl?"

He steps closer so the tips of his shoes are touching my bare toes. He tucks a finger beneath my chin, tilts it up and leans in close.

"If that's how you want it, then watch your tone, *Willow Girl*."

The low timbre of his voice is more warning than his words, and it takes all I have not to back off.

"Just tell me why. You owe me that much at least."

He steps back, giving me space to breathe.

"I thought you should know the stock you come from. And just to clarify, I don't owe you anything."

I ignore that last part.

"Well, don't you come from it too, considering you're descended from Anabelle Scafoni's son? Does that make us family? Cousins or something?" I don't know why I say it, it's so far in the past and so diluted, that it doesn't matter.

He grins, touches his middle finger to my collarbone, traces it to the hollow at my throat, up over it to my lips, presses until I open. When I close my teeth around the digit, he uses his finger like a hook and drags my face to his so we're nose to nose.

"You have got such a big mouth, you know that, Willow Girl?"

I reach into my pocket, feel the weight of the switchblade in it, pull it out.

He must hear it open. It's the only way he can react so quickly. The only way he can catch my hand before I can sink the little dagger into his gut.

I pull back to look down. He does the same. We watch the little drop of red stain the white of his dress shirt. He doesn't pull the blade back, though. He holds it there instead, even forces it a little, ripping his shirt, slicing his own flesh.

"Stop." There's a quiver in my voice. I try to pull my hand away, but he won't let me.

"Is that my notch?" he asks when he looks back up at me, holding my gaze as he relieves me of my weapon. I hear the clank of it when it hits the far wall. Before I can step back, his hand closes around my throat and he leans me backward over his desk, the angle painful.

One of my hands wraps around his forearm while the other one grips the edge of the desk to keep him from breaking my back.

"Do you know what would happen to you if you'd succeeded just now? What did I explain earlier?"

I know what he's talking about. That if he didn't do this, didn't take me, then his brother would or his brother after that.

"Let me go," I say.

His eyes are dark, black in the light, and I watch as he touches his wound with his fingers before bringing them to my thigh and smearing blood upward, pushing my underwear aside to rub it on my pussy, rub it inside me.

"You're always wet for me," he says before switching his grip to the back of my neck and kissing me hard, as hard as he's rubbing me. He breaks the kiss and watches me, and I hear him undo his jeans. He steps backward and pushed me to my knees.

I know what he wants.

He collects a fistful of my hair and grins. "Open up. I'm going to teach that big mouth a lesson."

I look up at him, try to pull back, but I can't.

He draws me up a little, painfully by my hair, and brings his face to mine. "If you bite, I'll whip you until I open your back, understand?" He squeezes that fistful of hair when I don't answer. "Do. You. Understand?"

"Yes!"

"That's a good Willow Girl. Now keep your eyes on mine, and open wide."

He doesn't even give me a minute to do it but pinches my nose closed, forcing my mouth open.

His cock is thick, hard, and ready. Precum tastes salty on my tongue as he moves me the way he wants, shallow at first, taking his time, watching me take him.

"First time?"

I don't say anything. I can't speak.

"Suck," he says as he pushes in deeper, and I do. I suck on his cock as he feeds it to me, deeper and deeper, tears forming at the corners of my eyes either from his hand fisting my hair too hard or from being choked on his cock. My voice, any words, are gargled as he hits the back of my throat and holds there for a moment, letting out a deep moan.

I push on his thighs and he pulls out a little, shallow again, pumping in and out slowly, going deeper; then, when I choke, shallow again.

"I like you like this, you know that? On your knees and quiet." He almost smiles. "Ready?"

Ready? Ready for what?

He forces my head forward, thrusting in to my throat.

I dig my fingers into his thighs and cry out, but the sound is muffled as he fucks my face, watching me as he takes me harder and harder until, finally, he stills inside me.

I feel the first spurt of cum hit the back of my throat and feel it slide down as the next one comes. I watch his face, and I hate that I can't look away, hate that he's so beautiful, hate that I want him even when I should hate him.

When he's emptied, he drops to his knees, breathing hard, smiling a little. He's still got hold of me, but he's not hurting anymore.

With his other hand, he pushes the hair that's stuck to the sheen of sweat on my forehead back.

He just looks at me for a minute before kissing me, kissing my mouth that tastes like him, that's just had him inside, that's just swallowed everything he gave me.

And when he slides one hand into my panties and rubs my clit, I kiss him back, and I come. I come on his fingers, in the palm of his hand, and I'm pulling him to me when I should be pushing him away.

Wanting him when I should be hating him.

11

SEBASTIAN

I'm up earlier than usual the next morning. Helena is fast asleep beside me, her arms hugged into her chest between us, forehead pressed against my shoulder.

It's funny, no matter how far from me she starts on the bed, every morning it's the same. She's curled so tight against me that I'm afraid to wake her when I get up.

She doesn't budge when I push the hair from her face to look at her. She looks younger than she is when she sleeps. It's because her face is so relaxed. She's always on her guard otherwise, and I understand that.

I get up, check my phone for a message I'm expecting. It's there, but I'm not sure if I'm happy about it or not. It could save Helena, if it comes to that, but it would destroy Ethan in the process.

I type a reply. I'll meet my contact in his Verona office the following day.

Helena doesn't move when I slip off the bed to have a shower, but when I come back into the bedroom, she's sitting up in bed, arms folded, her face like she's deep in thought. She turns to look at me, and I notice that she doesn't keep her eyes on mine.

"Good morning," I say.

"Why were the payments different when my Aunt Helena was the Willow Girl?"

I toss the towel I just used to dry my hair aside and step toward her, take her chin in my hand, and tilt her face up.

"I said good morning."

She looks at me, her forehead creasing. "Good morning."

"That's better. Why don't you go have a shower and get dressed? You should come downstairs for breakfast. You can't avoid my family forever."

"No, thanks. I'll lose my appetite with Ethan gawking at me."

"He can't help how he is, you know that, right?"

"What do you mean?"

"You must have noticed." Although she's had such little interaction with him, is it possible she hasn't?

She shrugs a shoulder. "He seems strange. I just thought he was a jerk."

"Oh, he is a jerk, but there's something else. He had an accident when he was fourteen. There was some damage to his brain."

"Oh."

I glance away, remembering, but only for a moment. "And Lucinda manipulates him. Teaches him everything he knows."

"Teaches him to hate me."

"Not just you. I'm just saying there's a reason he's the way he is. And that doesn't mean you should be alone with him, but just so you understand."

"It doesn't matter to me. He's still my enemy, no matter what. What was the accident?"

I turn away before answering. "A boating trip gone wrong." I walk into the closet to get dressed, pull on a pair of jeans. I have a T-shirt in my hands when I walk back into the bedroom to find her still on the bed.

She bites her lip. "So what happens when the year is up? I mean, do I just...do you... Do you stay here and I'm with him and..."

The thought of it, of handing her to him, of him touching her, makes my hands fist. Is it just her, or would I feel this way with anyone? I wouldn't wish my brother on any of the Willow Girls because it'd be handing her to Lucinda and handing her to Lucinda would be like handing her to Satan himself.

"Don't think about that now, Helena. There's a full year. A lot can happen."

"What does that mean?"

I pull my T-shirt on and go into the bathroom to comb my hair, but I'm really just buying time.

"You asked me about the payment when your Aunt Helena was the Willow Girl," I say, coming back into the bedroom.

She nods, sits up a little taller.

I sit on the edge of the bed. "How much do you know about her time here?"

"Not much. Only that she survived."

"She was here for two-and-a-half years. Not three."

"Why?"

"Because she killed the firstborn Scafoni son."

Helena's mouth falls open, and her eyes go wide. "What?"

"Smothered him in his sleep."

"How? I mean, she didn't say anything about that to me. Are you sure it's true?"

I nod. "Six months into her ordeal, she killed him, so she was passed on to the second. Then, after a year, to the third. That's why the discrepancy in payment."

"I don't believe you. This makes no sense. She's not a killer."

"She probably wouldn't be under normal circumstances."

"No. It's a mistake. It has to be."

"Funny thing was, his middle finger was missing, and they never found it."

At that, her eyes grow to twice their size.

"Helena, I'll admit, the bastard probably deserved what he got, but your aunt wasn't all there, and definitely not by the end."

"Did you think about what I asked? If I can call her?"

I get off the bed, walk to the dresser to put on my watch. "You want to ask her about this? Verify I'm not lying? She wouldn't tell you," I say, my back to her.

"Maybe because it's not true. Maybe it was one of his brothers. You're all ruthless. I don't see any brotherly love between any of you."

"Believe what you want. It's all written down. Recorded."

"Just because it's written down doesn't make it a fact."

I check my watch. "Go have a shower and come down to breakfast. I'll be there. You won't be alone."

She looks up at me, cocks her head to the side, and gives me a smirk. "Even if you're there, I'm still alone, Sebastian. More alone than I knew thanks to what I learned yesterday. And with today's story"—she shakes her head—"if you're trying to turn me against my family, it won't work."

"I'm just telling you the truth. Maybe think about the questions you ask me next time."

"You're unbelievable sometimes, you know that?" she says, sliding off the bed. She wraps the blanket around herself and turns to go into the bathroom.

I grab her arm, stop her. "And you wish you hated me for being a Scafoni, but you don't."

She tugs to free her arm, but I hold tight.

"Oh, I do hate you, Sebastian. I'll always hate you."

I stare at her, and she at me. The next time she tugs, I let her go.

She disappears into the bathroom and locks the door. That's why she showers here. The lock. It's probably why she sleeps in my bed.

Better the devil you know.

12

HELENA

I don't go downstairs to breakfast. I don't go for lunch either. I only make my way down when I'm too hungry to stay in my room.

I know Sebastian won't send food up. I also know he's right, that I have to face them sometime, but I'll put it off as long as possible.

The evening is cool and I wrap a sweater around myself. I'm the last to arrive. By the time I get out to the patio, the family is gathered around the table, Lucinda and Ethan drinking martinis, and Gregory and Sebastian, whiskey.

Two places are set for dinner, one in front of Sebastian and the other, Gregory, and Lucinda and Ethan are dressed in fancy evening wear. Maybe it's my lucky night and they're going out.

Sebastian is either bored or irritated. I can see it

on his face, in his posture. He sits opposite Lucinda, who has her back to me. He's leaning in his chair, head resting against the back, looking daggers at her until he sees me.

He shifts his gaze to me. I still can't read him, but I can't look away either. He does something to me. It's like when he's in a room, it's just him and me and every hair on my body stands on end. I don't know. It's like he steals the air out of my lungs.

I know the others feel this strange charge between us. They have to. And I can see from my periphery Ethan turning his head from me to Sebastian and back.

I told Sebastian that I hated him, and on some level, I do because he is my enemy. But I also know he is the one thing standing between me and the rest of them. I know they won't touch me as long as I have his protection.

It's not just that, though. I'm drawn to him. I want him. I want his hands on me. I want him inside me.

But the scariest part is that I want his arms around me when I sleep.

Lucinda slowly cranes her neck, and I clear my throat. The silence has become awkward.

"A drink?" I say.

Sebastian points to the long buffet table at the side where various drinks are laid out. I see a pitcher of martinis. I go to pour myself one, but a girl steps forward to do it for me. I watch her put three olives in a martini glass and pour the clear liquid. She hands it to me, and I sip. I feel it instantly, like the vodka is physically creeping down my shoulders.

I remember how Amy, the youngest of us, and I would sneak vodka when we could. Drink a little of it.

We started doing it the night my mother caught me with the boy when my father whipped me with his belt until I couldn't move anymore.

I still feel the shame of that night. The humiliation.

She had my sisters watch. A family punishment, after a proper family dinner. She had me strip naked from the waist down and bend over the recently cleared dinner table while they all watched.

At least she sent the maids out of the room.

When my father had thought I'd had enough, she ordered him to go on until welts covered me from the backs of my knees to the whole of my buttocks. A lesson for my sister's to learn what would happen should they try the same.

I think the Scafoni family is sick, but we're sick too, us Willows.

Amy's the only one of my sisters that I miss.

"You should teach your little pet to address us respectfully," Lucinda says, drawing me back into the present.

"I'll teach my pet to do as I like, not as you like."

I pick up a breadstick and turn, leaning my back against the buffet, crunching the breadstick and watching them silently, washing it down with my martini. I should take it easy. I haven't eaten all day.

It's breezy tonight, and Sebastian favors me in dresses apparently because that's about ninety percent of my wardrobe. I'm grateful the sleeves of my sweater are long, long enough I can hold them in my palms.

I lay one arm across my belly and just watch them while helping myself to a second breadstick.

Sebastian has turned his gaze back to Lucinda, and I guess they're having a staring contest that she's losing. I turn the bone ring in my hand, knowing now whose bone it is, feeling a surge of power run through me at the thought.

It's my secret. Just mine. I have a piece of them. My aunt took the finger of her Scafoni bastard, took the bone from it, and made it into an ornament for herself. A skull she hung around her neck like a token of her victory.

Her notch.

How fitting, the skull.

God, I want to laugh. I want to laugh out loud.

"Your aunt wasn't all there, and definitely not by the end."

Hell, maybe I'm not all there either because since I've come to this place, I feel insane.

Sebastian turns to me. He unceremoniously shoves out the chair beside his with his foot.

"Sit."

I guess those daggers are turned on me now. I walk obediently to the table and sit.

The girl I recognize from the few times she's been up to my room quickly sets a place before me.

"I'm hungry," Sebastian says. He's resumed his stare down of Lucinda.

She swallows the last of her drink and rises. Ethan follows her lead, and for the first time, I see the hesitation on his face and what Sebastian said makes sense. He's not all there. I'm curious what happened, what this accident was.

I glance at Sebastian. He's watching Ethan too, and I swear I see something like remorse there. But it's gone the instant Lucinda speaks.

"We'll be on our way, then. Don't want to keep you from your dinner."

She gives me a pointed look before she turns, and Ethan follows on her heels.

A few minutes later, I hear the engine of the boat just as a bottle of wine is opened and dinner is served, a steak for each of the brothers with a side of potatoes and roasted vegetables, and for me, the same, but instead of a beef steak, mine is a vegetarian version.

"Thank you," I say to the girl.

Sebastian and Gregory pick up their forks and cut into the meat. I start with a bite of potato. When I put the second bite into my mouth, Sebastian sits back and chews his, watching me.

He's in a mood.

"I want you down for every meal from now on."

"I don't eat breakfast," I say, knowing it's a weak excuse.

"Well, you'll start. Especially since we've taken into consideration your diet, and the cook is preparing special meals for you."

"Why are you taking it into consideration?"

"Christ. Can you ever just be grateful and move on?"

He's right on this one. I know it. "I am grateful. Thank you. It was just a question."

"Nothing is just a question with you. Eat. I don't want you too skinny."

"Not enough flesh to whip?"

"Something like that."

We glare at each other for a full minute until I can't anymore and do as he says. I eat. I'm starving, and the food is good.

I study Gregory while I work my way through my plate. He and Sebastian share similarities in features and, more so, mannerisms, and I can't help but watch them. They're not big on talking, so we eat mostly in silence.

"Were you both here when my Aunt Libby was the Willow Girl?"

They both look at me, and it's Sebastian who answers a moment later. "Yes, over the summers."

"What was she like?" They seem surprised by my question, and I clarify. "I was only five when she came home. I never really got to know her."

"She wasn't like you," Sebastian says.

"What does that mean?"

He continues like I haven't spoken at all. "Although by the time I met her, she'd spent six months on the island, so maybe she was like you in the beginning."

"Was it Lucinda who beat the marks into her back or was it your father?"

Gregory puts the last of his steak into his mouth, as if what I just asked was completely normal. All the while he's studying me, his eyes unreadable.

Sebastian wipes his mouth and puts his napkin on the table, finished with his meal.

"I saw them once," I say. "I still remember them. I thought they were tattoos. I had no idea."

"My father suffered after my mother's death. I don't know that he ever got over it. In a way, your aunt became a friend to him, and more," Sebastian says. "Lucinda hated her for that."

"That doesn't really answer my question." I look at Gregory.

"It was my mother who put those marks on your aunt's back," Gregory says.

I guess I didn't expect such a direct answer, especially from him because it's still his mother we're talking about. Maybe I don't expect him to speak to me at all. Every time he does, it's like he has to.

"Our father didn't stop her, which in my eyes, makes it as much his fault as hers," Gregory continues.

"Did you witness the punishments?"

"Some," Gregory answers.

"You didn't stop them either?"

"My brother was eight and I was twelve, Helena. We couldn't have stopped them if we wanted to," Sebastian replies.

"Did you want to?"

"Christ. Leave it alone," Sebastian says.

"She has a right to know if she wants to know, brother," Gregory says.

Sebastian turns to him. "But the problem, *brother*, is that Helena has a habit of asking questions she doesn't really want to know the answers to."

"I want to know," I say.

"Why?" Sebastian asks. "What purpose would it serve?"

"I can bear witness."

"Again, what purpose would it serve?"

"She has a right," Gregory repeats.

I turn to Gregory. "Do you want this? Do you want a turn with me?"

Sebastian snorts.

Gregory studies me for a long time before answering. "I know my duty as a Scafoni."

"But do you want it?"

"That's enough, Helena," Sebastian says. "Go to your room."

"I haven't had dessert." I retort as a girl appears with a tray of cakes.

Sebastian narrows his eyes at me but doesn't say anything when the girl comes to serve us. We eat the rest of the meal in silence.

When we're finished, Gregory pushes his chair back and walks out toward the pool, straddles one of the lounge chairs there, and takes out a pack of cigarettes. I guess I'm surprised he smokes when he lights one up and sits back to watch the night sky.

I feel Sebastian's gaze on me as I wipe my mouth and set my napkin on the table and stand.

"Sit."

"You were dismissing me a few minutes ago."

"And now I want you to sit. Or did you want to go chasing after my brother?"

I look at him, confused for a minute, but then I sit. A smile spreads across my face. It's not a nice smile.

"Are you jealous?" I cock my head to the side, make a point of studying him.

He leans in close, and it takes all I have not to lean away. "Be careful with my brother, Helena. He's not what you think. In fact, he's just as wicked as the rest of us."

He sits back in his seat, picks up the whiskey one of the girls brings him. They must know his habits by heart. He doesn't even have to lift a finger.

"I have no doubt. But you didn't answer my question," I say.

I know I'm playing with fire. This man calculates his every move, and he's much more adept at this game than I am.

"All right." He turns to the girls who are clearing. "Leave us."

Almost before he's finished saying it, they scatter away like mice, disappearing into the house. My heart falls to my stomach as he rises to his feet and I anticipate his punishment, because he will punish me for this.

"Up."

"Why? What are you going to do?"

"I'm going to give you what you want."

I glance over at the pool, to where Gregory is leaning back on the lounge chair, smoking his cigarette, blowing a circle of smoke up into the sky.

I shake my head no.

He gives me a smile. His isn't a nice one either. "Are you scared when I call your bluff, Willow Girl?"

I push my chair back, and the feet screech against the tiles.

Sebastian holds out his hand. His eyes give nothing away. I reach out to place my hand in his, and he walks me to the pool. I'm barefoot because I'd slipped my sandals off under the table. The grass between the tiled areas feels cool and soft beneath my feet.

Gregory turns to watch us, still smoking, casual, but something else too. Something darker that I hadn't noticed before.

I pull back, but Sebastian tugs me into his chest.

"Don't chicken out now, Willow Girl," he says, kissing my mouth.

I put my hands flat on his chest to push him off, but he cups the back of my head with one hand and won't release me from his kiss, although he doesn't slip his tongue into mine, not now.

But then I feel his other hand at my back, feel him unzipping my dress. He's still kissing me when he pushes the straps off my shoulders and down my arms so that I'm naked from the waist up.

I pull back, look over at Gregory, whose eyes are locked on me.

"What are you doing?" I ask Sebastian, my voice quieter, my throat suddenly dry.

In answer, he kisses me again, kisses my cheek, then my mouth and pushes the dress off so I'm just in my underwear.

"Sebastian." I shove against him, but to no avail.

"You want my brother?"

I shake my head and glance back, but Gregory hasn't moved, and his dark eyes are locked on me. On us.

Is he going to share me?

Is he going to give me to his brother?

Sebastian's eyes narrow, and this notch is his. He knows it as well as I.

"You've made your point. Stop," I say.

But he doesn't.

Instead, he turns me so that my back is to him and I'm facing Gregory. He slides his big hand into the front of my panties and cups my pussy while the fingers of his other hand find my nipple and knead.

Gregory's eyes lock on mine, and I can't look away. Can't look away as he watches me in this most vulnerable position.

"You're wet, Helena," Sebastian whispers at my ear.

I feel his hardness behind me and from here, I can see that Gregory is aroused too. There's a moment when I wonder if they'll both have me at once. It excites me as much as it terrifies me. And this, Sebastian letting his brother watch me, I know it's a trap but also my punishment.

All the while, Sebastian's working me slow. He must feel me when I'm close, and he backs off again and again. His mouth is on my neck, kissing me, and like a child who closes her eyes when she wants to hide, I shift my face from Gregory's, unable to look at him.

But then he moves, and I turn to see him straddling the chair, legs wide, thighs powerful, and he's stubbing out his cigarette.

He gets up and comes over and stands inches from me. His cock is hard, like a rod straining against his jeans. I swallow when Sebastian pulls his hand for my panties, leaving me unsatisfied, leaving a wet trail across my belly.

Gregory's gaze slides down over my belly, and I press back against Sebastian. Sebastian takes my wrists and holds them at my sides when Gregory reaches out and touches me, runs the fingernails of one hand over my breast, his gaze never leaving mine as he slides his hand inside my panties where Sebastian's just was.

"Stop," I try.

His fingers feel foreign. Rough.

I twist this way and that, but Sebastian's got me tight. Gregory's rubbing my pussy, working my clit, and I don't want this. I don't.

God, I don't.

And even as I deny it, I feel the tension building, feel my body preparing. I'm going to come. One more second, and I'm going to come. That sound, it's me, it's my breath hitching too loud in this quiet night.

"Enough," Sebastian commands from behind me.

I meet Gregory's eyes again when he stops, drags his hand from inside my panties, and smears my own juices across my belly, just like his brother did.

He then turns and walks away, walks back to the patio, pours himself a whiskey, and sits down.

He watches us as Sebastian pushes me down on my knees and kneels behind me. He switches his grip, dragging my arms in front of me, taking both wrists into one of his hands and with the other, turning my face so I can see him from the corner of my eye.

"Not what you wanted?"

I jerk my face away. He pushes my panties down, and I hear him unzip his jeans. A moment later, he's inside me, thrusting once, twice, before he pulls out.

"You're dripping," he whispers at my ear, and I feel him grip my ass, slip his fingers between my cheeks, and finger my pussy. He then slides his fingers into my asshole and rubs.

"Sebastian," I say, understanding his intention. Unable to drag my eyes from the outline of where Gregory sits, watching us. "I didn't mean—"

He pushes a finger inside my ass, and I gasp. He keeps it there and tugs me closer, so my back is flat to his chest.

"You're mine, Helena. *Mine*."

He pulls his finger out and pushes me forward,

releasing my wrists so I'm on hands and knees. He pushes his cock into my pussy again, once, twice, then pulls out. I feel him at my back hole.

He grips my hip with one hand while sliding the other to my clit. I cry out when he pushes against me, against my ass with his too thick, too big cock.

"I can't. You can't—" I try to crawl away, but his fingers dig into my hip.

"I am. If you relax, it'll go easier."

"Please don't."

He pulls back, rubs my clit, and I don't know if I hate myself or him more because I'm going to come. After this humiliation, I'm going to fucking come. He knows it and I know it, and there's nothing I can do to stop it and Gregory is still sitting there watching us, sipping his drink and just watching us.

When it happens, when I come, he pushes into my ass. It hurts, and I'm coming all at once.

It's like tumbling from one orgasm to the next, and the sensations overlap, pain and ecstasy and pain, repeating, repeating like the pattern of the strangling, choking roses on my walls, as he penetrates deeper, taking more of me, claiming more of me as orgasm rocks my body.

He hauls me upright, my back to his front, and he's all the way inside me. I can feel every inch of him. He wraps one hand around my throat, and the other is cupping my pussy.

"Mine, Helena. Every part of you is mine," he

says, fucking my ass in quick, deep, punishing thrusts, rubbing me again until I'm coming again and he's coming too, and his brother is still watching and Sebastian is filling me up and holding me tight and repeating that one word over and over and over again until I know that I am his.

Only his.

13

HELENA

He doesn't carry me to his bed that night. Instead, he brings me to my own room and sets me on the bed on my belly. He goes into the bathroom and returns a moment later with a washcloth. When I realize what he means to do, I capture his wrist, try to get up.

"I can do it."

"Lay back down."

"Please."

He raises an eyebrow. I lay down again and turn my face away, bury it in the sheets when he pulls me apart to clean me, clean his cum coming out of me.

He's so gentle, and it's so humiliating. More so than the act itself. More than his brother watching. He doesn't speak a word when he does it. When he's finished, he disappears into the bathroom. The water goes on. He's back a few minutes later.

I sit up on the bed, pull my knees into me.

"Why did you do that?" I can't look at him.

"Which part? The part where I let my brother touch you? Or the part where I fucked your ass? Or was it that I let him watch?"

I give a shake of my head and turn my face to the windows because I'm going to cry again, and I can't anymore. I can't let him see me cry again. See how easily he hurts me.

Hurt me.

Why does this hurt me? Injure me?

"Which part, Helena?"

I let out a breath. "No part." I turn to look up at him. "I'm tired."

"Then I'll leave you to sleep. You'll be down to breakfast at nine tomorrow morning, and you'll have an overnight bag packed to leave directly after."

"Overnight?"

"I have to be in Verona. I'm taking you with me. Good night, Helena."

He uses the connecting door between our rooms, which he closes but doesn't lock.

I draw the blankets back, not having the energy to get up, put on a nightie, or anything. I slip beneath them and turn my back to the door and watch the night sky through the open windows. I pull the blankets up to my chin and try to think of anything else but what just happened because I can't think about it right now. I can't analyze it. I'm too afraid of what I'll find.

THE NEXT MORNING, I WAKE TO THE SOUND AND SMELL of rain.

I open my eyes and push the covers back. When I sit up, I remember what we did last night. How he had me. How Gregory touched me. How he watched.

I'm embarrassed and turned on and, god, I don't even know. It's confusing and almost overwhelming, all of this.

But I can't let him overwhelm me. I can't let him because I can't weaken. Is that what he wants? To weaken me? To break me? He told me as much, right? This is a game to him. And for every game, for there to be a winner, there has to be a loser.

I have no doubt Sebastian will win this.

I check the clock someone put in here a few days ago, and it's half past eight. I get up, walk to the window. The sky is dark with clouds as far as I can see. I hate rain. I hate the darkness that comes with it. I always have. But today, it fits my mood. Fits this place.

I go into the bathroom to have a shower and choose yet another dress, this one a light-pink cotton almost knee-length dress with short sleeves, buttons all the way down the front and cinched at the waist. I grab a sweater to go with it and choose a pair of white, flat sandals. The color is pretty with my hair, which I gather into a messy bun at the top of my head so it doesn't soak the back of the dress while it dries.

I set some things on the bed to take with me, but I don't have a bag to pack, so I just leave it and head down to breakfast at a few minutes before nine.

Sebastian makes a point of checking his watch when I arrive. The family is already gathered, everyone but Ethan, eating their breakfast.

"Good morning," Sebastian says.

I clear my throat and am relieved when my voice doesn't break when I reply. "Morning." It's not necessarily a good one.

"Sleep well?" he continues. I can feel everyone's focus on me, and I want to make a point of looking at each of them, of showing them I'm not a coward, but I can't.

"Fine," I say tightly.

His eyes are studying me. He's keeping me rooted to the spot, not dismissing me to get my breakfast, because he can. Because he wants me to know he can.

I already know this, though.

I know he holds power over every aspect of my life, and I feel a wave of sadness at the thought.

What did I think? That it would be different?

How many days have I been here? Already, look at me.

What a fool I am to think I could beat him. Beat them.

"Get your breakfast," he says, finally dismissing me.

It's just in time, because when I turn away, I can pretend I'm scratching my cheek and wipe away a misguided tear.

I'm not hungry. I don't think I could get anything past the lump in my throat if I tried, but I fill a plate and pour myself a cup of coffee. I even forego the cream because I just can't think this morning.

Their eyes are on me, and I wonder if they talk when I'm not there or if they truly do hate each other.

I take my seat, the same one as last night. My shoes are still there. And I don't need to glance at the pool to know that the soaked pile of a dress and panties are mine.

Did he do that on purpose? More humiliation? Last night wasn't enough?

I pretend to busy myself with breakfast and manage a forkful of scrambled eggs, but it's like I'm swallowing rocks.

"I came downstairs for my morning swim before this wretched rain. I didn't appreciate seeing your dirty underwear by the pool, Willow Girl," Lucinda taunts, biting loudly into a piece of overtoasted toast.

I fist my fork, wondering if I'd make it to stab her in the eye before anyone stops me. It'd be worth a round at the whipping post.

I eat another bite.

"I hope you weren't swimming naked. That's disgusting."

I suck a slow breath in and swivel my head in her direction. "Actually, I wasn't swimming at all. I was getting fucked. Something you might consider doing. If you can find someone willing to touch you, of course. It might make you less of a bitch."

Her face goes red, and a genuine smile stretches my lips. I turn back to my plate and cut into the stack of two pancakes. I see Sebastian straighten and cover his mouth with a napkin and hear his chuckle.

Lucinda slams her fist on the table. "Are you going to allow this?"

I look up at the wrong moment because Gregory's eyes are the ones I meet, and I feel my face heat up, going red.

"You asked, Lucinda. She was just clarifying. And in Helena's defense, it's my fault the clothes are still there. She couldn't walk after the fucking, could you?" He touches my hand with the tips of two fingers.

I look at his fingers on me, drag my gaze to his face to take in the satisfied grin.

"No. You're *that* good," I say.

It's Gregory who snorts a short laugh this time.

Lucinda shoves her chair back and comes toward me. For a moment, I wonder if she's going to slap me.

"Lucinda," Sebastian's voice is a quick command, and she, remarkably, obeys, stopping just a few steps from me.

I meet her gaze, unable to help the small gleam of victory I feel.

"You'll pay for that, Willow Girl. I'm patient, but I will have my turn."

It takes all I have to keep my expression neutral because I do believe she means it. She will have her turn at me.

She walks away a moment later. Sebastian leans back in his chair, his eyes burning a hole through me.

"You're owed a notch," he says, finishing the last of his coffee. "Are you packed?"

"I didn't have a bag, so I put the things I want to take on my bed."

He nods and calls a girl over, tells her to pack my things into his bag. It's quiet while I force the rest of my breakfast down.

"A word of advice," says Gregory, and I am forced to look up at him. All I can think of is how he looked at me last night. How he touched me. How he watched us. Watched me come. "Don't taunt my mother. She has nothing better to do than hate you."

"Am I just expected to sit here and be humiliated? Morning and night?"

"You are the Willow Girl," he says.

"I don't care what you do to me. What she does to me. I can't—I won't—just take it. I'm not that kind of Willow Girl."

"You're all that kind of Willow Girl by the end," he says.

I touch the bone ring on my finger and will myself to be strong. To have just a little bit of my Aunt Helena's strength.

But they are wearing me down. Slowly and surely, whittling me down to bare bone. I wonder if they'll make a notch out of me.

A prize.

"Finished?" Sebastian asks.

I guess I'm staring at Gregory, processing his words. Remember Sebastian's: *"Be careful with my brother, Helena. He's not what you think. In fact, he's just as wicked as the rest of us."*

A chill makes me shudder.

I set my fork and knife at a diagonal across my plate and turn to Sebastian. He's watching me with his slate eyes, and I swear he knows every thought in my mind. Knows my every weakness.

"Yes."

He rises and pulls my chair out. I'm surprised by the politeness.

"We'll leave in fifteen minutes," he says and disappears into the house.

I reach under the table to pick up my abandoned

sandals from last night and dart to the pool in the rain to scoop up my clothes before heading back into the house, drenched. But before I get past him, Gregory grabs my wrist and stops me. He looks up at me from his seat, lets his gaze run over me before looking me in the eye.

"I mean it. Be careful with my mother."

I swallow. "I'm not scared of her."

I try to pull free, but he rises to his feet, keeping me close, bruising my wrist. We're so close, I have to crane my neck to look up at him.

"What about me? Are you scared of me?"

I guess I'm not expecting that, and I guess I've given him the reaction he wants. That deer in the headlights look.

He gives me a grin, then releases me and goes inside. When I'm alone, I sink down into the closest chair because my knees give out.

Did I think for a second last night that Gregory would come to my rescue? I did. I did for a split second. But I have to remember that no one's coming to my rescue.

No one but me.

14

SEBASTIAN

I don't mind the rain. I like it. It's a nice change of pace.

The drive to Verona takes twenty minutes longer than the hour and fifteen minutes it should because idiots don't know how to drive in rain, but our hotel is dry and our suite has a great view of the city.

I'm unpacking some things from our overnight case when Helena comes out of the bathroom drying her face. She looks around, and I wonder if she notices the lack of telephones. I made sure they were removed before we got here.

She's been quieter than usual this morning. I expect it's because of last night, and I guess that was my point. Bring her down a notch.

She sits down on the edge of the bed like she's exhausted. "What are we doing here?"

"I have a meeting this afternoon, and I thought you might like to get off the island at least for a night."

She looks around, scoots back a little on the bed. She's taken off her sweater. When she reaches to brush the hair out of her eyes, I notice the bruises forming on her wrist. She follows my gaze. She must have noticed them herself because she closes her hand over them and rubs.

"Can't tell who leaves the marks anymore, can you?"

I can see she's on edge.

"I can't," she continues. "You. Your brother. Your stepmother. All I know is it's like playing a game. I'm the punching bag, and you all just keep taking turns, one after the other after the other, just beating on me while you have a grand old time."

I take her arm to look at her wrist. "Gregory?"

She doesn't respond, but I know.

"When did he touch you?"

"You mean after you allowed him to last night? After you offered me to him last night? After you let him watch?"

I look at her, and I know I have to keep myself reined in. I see it all over her face. She's barely holding it together.

"When, Helena?"

"This morning. After you left."

"Did you provoke him?"

"Provoke him?" She pulls her arm back. "I didn't. But even if I did, in your family, if a girl provokes one of you, she earns the bruises? They're her fault?"

"What happened?"

"So, let me be sure I understand," she continues. "By your logic, if a girl is walking on a street at night, is it her fault if she's attacked? Or do these rules only apply to the unlucky Willow Girls?"

I draw in a long, slow breath and count to ten. "He has no right to touch you."

"Of course, he does. You let him, remember? You *invited* him to touch me."

"Last night was different."

"Because *you* were putting me in my place. Not him. Is that it with you? Only you can punish me? Hurt me?"

"Be careful."

"You like hurting me. You said so."

She looks down, begins to pick at a cuticle. I see her forehead crease, and it takes her a minute to smooth it out again.

"I know you're not my friend. I know you're not my ally, even if you say you are, but even when you hurt me, I know you're not really going to hurt me." She gets up, puts her hand to her forehead, and crosses the room. "God, that's dumb." She turns to me, and the delicate skin around her eyes is red. "I guess I'm not as much a challenge as you thought, huh?" Her voice breaks, and she wipes tears from her eyes.

I go to her, take her wrists, pull her hands from her face. "Helena—"

She slaps my arms away, steps back. Her eyes are fierce through the tears. "Don't you mean *Willow Girl*?"

I take hold of her arms, back her against the wall. She doesn't fight me.

"I think the hardest part is that I don't understand why some stupid part of me keeps thinking or hoping you'll save me even when I know you won't," she says.

She's coming apart, and all I can do is watch her. Stand there, mute, watching her. Because what can I tell her?

"You like this, right? When I cry?" she continues.

"Not like this." I touch her face, take it into my hands. I feel like I'm always wiping tears from her eyes. I lean in and kiss her, holding her, just kissing her, trying to pull her to me.

She makes a sound, tries to push away, but I kiss her harder.

"Stop," she says when I draw back, when I undo the top buttons of her dress, and pull it over her head. "Stop." She pushes me away.

"Shh, let me take care of you, Helena."

She shakes her head, but it's a weak effort. When

I reach behind her to unhook her bra, her fight is halfhearted.

"It's like you said," she says when I pull the straps off her arms and stand back to look at her. "My body wants it. You were right. You keep winning. You keep collecting the notches."

"No notches." I take her face in my hands again, tilt it up, and make her look at me. "Not tonight. Not here, okay?"

I kiss her again, then lift her in my arms, lay her on the bed, and drag her panties from her before stripping off my own clothes. Keeping most of my weight on my forearms, I slide into her, watching her feel me, so close to her that it's not possible to get closer.

She opens her mouth a little wider, and her breath hitches as I stretch her.

"Fuck, Helena. You feel so good. So fucking good."

I've only fucked her up until now, but this, being inside her now, warm and tight and safe, it's different. It's slow and deep and as close to making love as I have ever or will ever get.

I've never made love before. I've never wanted to. I've never wanted to be that close to anyone. But right now, with her like this, vulnerable and breaking a little, fracturing before my eyes, I want to make love to her.

"Sebastian—"

"Shh. Just you and me. Here. Now. No Willow daughter. No Scafoni son. Just you and me."

She stares up at me. I kiss her mouth again. She's so soft and so sweet when she's not fighting me. I know she wants this too. I know she wants it like this, who we are erased. The past absent. Just us.

I kiss her cheek, her jaw, her throat, that delicate hollow between her collarbones. Her hands are on me, on my shoulders, then in my hair. Her legs wrap around my hips when I bring my face to hers, watching her as I fuck her deep and slow. She's wet and tight and fuck, I love being inside her.

Taking one of her legs, I open it wide, bending it at the knee so I can see her, see her taking me, and go deeper still because I can't get deep enough with her. I can't get close enough.

"I'm going to come," she whispers against my mouth, closing her eyes.

"Look at me. I want to see you. I want to see you come like this."

She opens her eyes. Her hands are on either side of my face, and I'm fucking her deep, each thrust closer to her center, each thrust cleaving us together, and she doesn't come like she does when I fuck her hard. This is different, a gradual building of tension, a wave, not a tsunami. I watch her, watch how soft her eyes go, her face, watch her as I feel her squeezing around me. Hear the sigh of her breath. It takes all I have not to come too, not to empty inside her.

Lifting her, I shift our position so I'm sitting against the headboard and she's straddling my lap. Our eyes lock. I grip her hair, pull her to me, kiss her before shifting on hand to her hip, moving her over me.

She claws my shoulders, and I watch her when I kiss her. I need her like this right now. I need all of her. My cock in her pussy, my tongue in her mouth, my hands on her, holding her tight to me.

Fuck.

I tighten my grip on her hair and drive deeper into her.

I'm rough with her, and when I tug her head back, she cries out, coming again, coming harder than before, milking my dick as I keep her speared, feel her throb, her cunt pulsating around my cock, her breath warm in my mouth.

I watch her as I empty inside her. As I hold her close and just watch her because I can't stop fucking wanting her.

Rain comes down in sheets outside. Spent, I cradle Helena in the crook of my arm. We're quiet for a long time as she rests against me. I like it, I like her like this. Like us like this.

"I know why you sleep in my room. Why you shower there. I know it's that you're safest from the others there. I know it's not me."

She shifts a little to look up at me.

"But you know what you do at night?" I ask.

I look down at her. I don't know why I'm telling her, but looking at her like this, seeing what I see in her eyes, I have to. I have no choice.

"You curl into me," I continue. "Always. It's not that you hold on to me. You don't. You curl up into my chest, but you don't quiet until I put my arms around you and cocoon you."

She smiles, looks away for an instant then turns back to me. "Do you know how creepy that sounds? That you watch me sleep?"

I look at her midnight eyes. "You have the prettiest, saddest eyes I've ever seen."

At that, she pulls away, but I don't let her go. I hold tighter, and she buries her face in my shoulder.

"You shouldn't talk to me like this," she says.

"Why not?"

She turns her head to meet my eyes. "Because I..." She stops, blinks, scrunches up her forehead, then seems to change her mind. She scoots off my lap and draws the covers up to her chest.

"Because no matter what, Sebastian, you are a Scafoni and I am a Willow. We aren't friends. We're enemies. You will destroy me inch by inch, and it's easier...I have a chance...if I hate you. And this, what just happened, you touching me like that, talking to me like that, like I'm not just the Willow Girl..."

Her lip trembles, and tears fall from her face and

one lands on my forearm. I almost look away from her to watch that drop slide over my skin. Almost.

"Like you care," she says.

It's quiet again, but something is building inside her. I see it. Feel it.

She shakes her head, slips off the bed and I let her go. She takes the blanket with her, holds it against her chest, hiding herself from me.

"It can't ever happen again, Sebastian, because I can't care about you."

15

HELENA

After swearing our conversation wasn't over, Sebastian left for his meeting.

I'm sitting in the hotel room watching the sun curl around an angry cloud, promising more rain to come.

He'll be gone for several hours. I'm surprised he left me unsupervised. Even allowed me to go anywhere I like—as long as it's inside the hotel. Eat something, buy something from the boutique, and just charge it to the room.

Christ, I feel like a child. I don't even have a dollar to buy myself a cup of coffee.

I look around the large living room and realize there isn't a telephone in here, not even on the desk. I get up and search the bedroom. There are phone jacks, but no phone. I snort, remembering how on our way up here, we'd passed a housekeeper's cart.

I'd noticed the two telephones with their cords wrapped around them on top of a stack of towels. I'd thought it was strange, but it hadn't really registered then that he probably had the hotel remove the phones before we arrived.

I shake my head. All that sweet talk. All that lovemaking. More Scafoni bullshit. But he made a mistake, leaving me here.

He unpacked the overnight bag before he left. I go to the closet and open the door. Like the obsessive neat freak he is, I see he's hung up our things. A suit for him, a pair of jeans, a dress for me. Our shoes are neatly lined up on the floor, mine next to his like we're just a normal couple. Like we're here on some lovers' getaway.

Is that what he thinks this is? Is he pretending that's what we are?

I reach into the pockets of his suit jacket as well as the dress slacks but come up empty. His jeans, though, turn up a wad of bills. Not a huge amount, about €90. Not enough to do anything significant, but something.

It's not like him to stuff bills into his pocket. Maybe he did it when we stopped for gas and he bought himself a cup of coffee and me a bottle of water. I take the money, put on the raincoat Sebastian had the presence of mind to bring for me because I hadn't packed one, and head downstairs.

In the lobby, I see a telephone. I start for it but

then stop, remembering it's the middle of the night at home. I can't call yet, but I will. I have no idea what I'll say, but I will call.

I bypass the restaurant and the gift shop and step outside, hesitating on the stairs of the beautiful hotel, knowing I'm breaking his rule.

What am I even doing? Running away?

I shake my head and turn back, even take a step back inside the hotel entrance, but I can't. I can't just give in. Give up.

And so, without thinking about where I'm going or what I'm doing, if I'm coming back before he gets back or if I'm disappearing, I walk out of the hotel and into the beautiful city not seeing a thing, too deep in thought.

One thing I can't stop thinking about is how I know that no matter what happens to me, my sisters will continue this tradition when it comes their turn. They will dress their daughters, my nieces, in those rotting, yellowing sheaths and put them on those horrible blocks to be looked over, judged, touched by the next Scafoni bastard. Put there for him to take his pick. Like we're not human. Like we're animals.

I guess we are to them.

My thoughts jump back to what just happened between us. To him talking to me like he did, holding me like he did. Making love to me. It's the only time I've been made love to.

The first time I had sex, the only time before Sebastian, the boy and I were both sixteen. Kids. Neither of us knew what we were doing, and the only reason I did it at all was because I needed him to rip through that thin sliver of flesh that marked me a virgin.

It didn't feel good. In fact, I remember it hurt, but I gritted my teeth and tried to block out his wet, panting breath at my ear. He'd used a condom, and he'd come quickly with a little grunt. I remember I wanted him off me as soon as it was over.

It's very different with Sebastian. I want sex with Sebastian. And it's not just my body betraying me. It's me wanting to be close to him.

And this is what scares me the most.

I give a violent shake of my head. It's so out of place that the people passing me stop and stare. I only half meet their eyes but hug the coat to myself and walk on.

I can't think about that. I can't think about him making love to me. Touching me gently or roughly. I can't think about what he said, that he watches me sleep. that I curl into him, that he cocoons me. Shelters me. I know that already, and I can't go there.

But then again, maybe it's my dependence on him that makes this so strange. That confuses my feelings so completely.

I think about my Aunt Libby and wonder, for the first time, if she wasn't heartbroken when she came home. If she didn't kill herself because of missing her Scafoni master. Because maybe this is what they do. Maybe we become so helplessly dependent on them that we think we love them.

I wander around for a while, not sure where I'm going, and only notice I'm out of the center when I realize the streets aren't as busy here and the shops are local shops, markets and a dentist, a beauty salon. A run-down antique shop stuffed so full that the faces of the dolls smashed against the window watch me creepily as I walk by.

When the rain starts back up, I duck into one of the shops and use Sebastian's money to buy an umbrella. Back outside, I watch people rush by, some with giant umbrellas, some on bikes, and tourists dragging their oversize suitcases along uneven, rain-soaked streets. I listen to their complaints about the weather and I think they should be grateful. They're free. How we take simple freedoms for granted. How I did.

A car drives too fast to make the traffic light, splashing water on my legs. I look up, mentally curse the driver, and realize why there are so many people with suitcases here.

I'm at the Verona train station.

When the light changes, I cross the street, avoiding the bigger puddles, and run under the cover of the overhanging roof of the station, shaking out my umbrella and closing it before walking inside. It's busy here and loud with people waiting out of the rain.

I reach into my pocket, feeling the stack of bills, and read the schedule boards. There's a train leaving for Rome in thirty minutes, and a ticket will cost me €65.

I walk toward the counter. I even get in line. But there's a part of me that wonders what I'm doing. What I will do. Where will I go? Home? How? With what money? What passport? Besides, my parents won't want me back. Given what I've learned, I wouldn't put it past them to return me to the Scafoni family.

The line moves, and it's my turn. I take out my wad of borrowed bills. "Rome, please. One-way."

What am I doing?

The woman says something I don't understand between the noise around me, my own thoughts, and her accent, but she points to the screen displaying the amount I owe.

I push my money into the little tray under the glass. A few minutes later, she spins it around. I take my change and my ticket and step out of the line. Someone bumps into me, or truly, I bump into them because I'm not paying attention.

"I'm sorry."

The man barely gives me a sideways glance and carries on talking into his cell phone, rushing to his train.

I head to the turnstiles. I'm just following those ahead of me. I have no identification. No passport. No nothing. Just a little more than €20 in my pocket and my train ticket.

A crowd of people rushes past me. They're panicked, like they're about to miss their train, and I step aside to let them pass.

I have half an hour, so I walk across the station to the coffee shop and order an espresso at the bar. I stand with the locals and take the tiny cup of thick black liquid and sip it. It's too strong. I try again but put the cup down and look at the check under the cup for what I owe. I reach into my pocket and pull out the handful of coins from the umbrella purchase. I'm rifling through them, turning each one over to see what's what when an arm slides around my waist.

I shift my gaze to the fingers that curl around me, and I'm not sure if I'm surprised.

I look up at him.

He's not looking at me.

Before I've made sense of my coins, Sebastian drops three on the counter and picks up the train ticket next to my coffee cup. I watch him read it and realize that drumbeat is my heart pumping blood loudly in my ears. He reads the ticket, crumples it in his fist, and shoves it into his jacket pocket.

When he finally looks at me, his eyes are dark. He doesn't speak, not a word, and if there's one thing

I've learned about him, it's that when he's truly angry, he's quiet. He's thinking. Planning the best mode of attack.

"Finish your coffee."

"I-I'm finished."

He picks up my tiny espresso cup, hands it to me. My hands shake when I take it from him. I don't think he blinks while I force down the too dark coffee.

When I'm finished, he nods, takes the cup, and puts it back onto its saucer.

I expect we'll leave right away, but we don't. We stand at the bar, my back to it while he faces it, his arm now around my front, fingers still gripping my waist. He's watching me, and I'm watching the people move around us, most rushing, some strolling, stopping for coffee, sitting at a table to eat something.

The noise of the station fades into the background, the announcements, the rain, the chatter. Sebastian takes a deep breath in, and I turn to him.

"I don't understand you," he says.

I stare back at him. I want to ask what he doesn't understand. I want to ask how he found me. I want to ask how angry he is.

No, not that last one. I can see that. It's in the tightening of his chiseled jaw. In the hardening of his full lips.

Lips that kissed me gently and spoke sweetly just a few hours ago.

Gentleness and sweetness that I rejected.

"You prefer me to be rough with you? Is that it?" His fingers dig into my skin. "You choose to draw a line between us?"

"It's not a choice. None of this has ever been a choice for me."

His eyes scan my face, narrow a little.

"I can be rough with you, if that's what you want," he says quietly. Calmly. "What you need."

I swallow. I know he means it.

Without another word, he shifts his grip to my hand, fist on fist, squeezing so hard my fingernails cut into my skin. He picks up my umbrella—I'd forgotten it—and like this, not quite hand in hand, we walk out of the station and into the rain, to the line of waiting taxis. He opens the back door of the first one and gestures for me to get in. I do. He follows and gives the driver an address in Italian.

About ten minutes later, ten minutes where he doesn't speak a single word, ten minutes where I feel his anger throbbing like a separate entity in the car, we pull up to a shop. It looks like men's shoes.

He gives the driver some instruction before opening the door of the taxi, not bothering with the umbrella as he drags me out with him. In the distance, I can see blue skies, but here, rain is pouring down.

A bell rings over the door as we enter, opera music playing softly, the faint scent of a cigar having been smoked recently filtered by that of leather and expensive cologne. The older man who is reading the paper behind his desk looks up at Sebastian, smiles in recognition, stands.

Sebastian speaks a few words to him. His tone is clipped.

The man's smile turns into a nod and a quick glance at me. He disappears behind a curtain.

Sebastian is still squeezing my fist, and his hand feels hot.

A few minutes later, the man reappears with a thin cord of leather about three feet long. Sebastian releases my hand, takes it, wraps it around his fist and tests its strength.

When I look up at the old man, he quickly looks away. Sebastian says something to him, tucks the cord into his pocket, hands him some bills, and, a few minutes later, we're in the taxi again and heading back into the center of Verona and to our hotel. By the time we arrive the rain has turned into a drizzle, but the city is drenched, even the sunlight is a dampened yellow.

Sebastian pays the driver. We leave the umbrella when we walk back into the hotel and at the front desk, he asks for the key. They still use the old-fashioned ones you turn in when you leave. We head up to our suite and, once inside, he finally releases me.

I step away, look at the crescent indents my fingernails carved into my palm, look back at him. "Are you going to talk to me?"

He takes off his jacket, hangs it up, takes that corded-up leather out of the pocket and sets it on the table beside the door along with the room key with its red tassel hanging from it.

"Take off your jacket and hang it up."

I do as he says and hang it beside his. He looks me over.

"Your shoes too."

I look down, slide off the shoes which have tracked dirt into the room, and instantly lose two inches.

"Let's go into the bedroom."

"Why?" I'm cautious. He's not going to just let this go.

"Because I said so."

When I don't move, he comes to me. I expect him to grip my arm and make me go. But instead his fingertips are gentle at my low back. I walk into the bedroom with him.

He goes to the full-length mirror against the far wall, moves a chair to clear a large space, then turns to me.

"Come here."

I do. I stand with my back to the mirror facing him. He looks at me again, at the buttons of my dress. I'm still when he begins to undo them, one by one, taking care not to touch my skin when he does.

"What are you going to do?" I ask quietly because he will punish me. I know it.

He meets my eyes, then shifts his gaze back to the buttons, unbuttoning each one carefully, taking his time until the dress is undone to just below my waist. He pushes it open a little, just enough to glimpse the swell of my breasts in my lace bra. Leaving me there, he walks into the living room and returns with the leather cord.

"Do I need to tie you?"

I look at it, unsure what he's planning. Is he going to tie me up with it?

"What are you going to do?" I ask again.

"Do I need to tie you?" he repeats.

I slowly, uncertainly, shake my head no.

"Good."

He reaches out, pushes the hair that rain stuck to my forehead away, looks at me and for a minute, I regret what I did. I regret rejecting him. I regret running off.

"I wasn't going to get on the train." I wasn't. It's true.

"I know." He touches my cheek like he's wiping something off, then meets my eyes again. "Turn around."

"You don't have to punish me."

But he does. And he will. His silence tells me so.

"Why?" I ask. I feel myself begin to tremble. Feel the heat of tears building behind my eyes.

"Turn around, Helena. Do as I say. It's important you do as I say."

I turn slowly so I'm facing the mirror. I don't look at us, not right away. Instead, I look at the reflection of the window, see how the shadows are growing long outside as evening slowly descends. I must have been gone for hours.

It's when I feel his hands on me that I watch him. They're on my shoulders, and he squeezes them, rubs them. Wraps his big hands around them. I want to lean into him, I want to take back what I said and lean into his powerful chest and let him hold me. Not punish me.

But his fingers take hold of my open dress and slowly, gently, so carefully, drag it over my shoulders, not off, only halfway down my arms. He does the same with the straps of my bra. His hands burn my skin as he collects my hair and lifts the mass of it to set it over my shoulder before kissing it.

His lips are soft against my skin.

"You're perfect," he says to my reflection.

I turn my head, my cheek almost touches his. The scruff of his jaw is rough. He's warm. I almost turn around, but he must sense it and he shakes his head a little. His hands are on my arms, rubbing them.

"I'm going to punish you, Helena."

My tears begin to fall like the rain of the afternoon.

I nod my head. I know he's going to punish me. And I know it's going to be bad. Not like before. Not like when he used his belt. This will be worse because it means more now.

"And I don't want you to fight me. I don't want to tie you. It's important."

I nod again, stupidly, and his hands come to the tops of my shoulders. He puts a little pressure on them.

"Kneel."

There's a moment of panic, but he's behind me, pressing against me, arms around me holding me to him. One hand covers one breast and squeezes it, weighs it, while the other slips under my dress, fingertips sliding into my panties, just touching my clit. I watch us like this, my lips slightly parted.

This is what I look like when I want.

"Kneel, Helena."

I nod. I don't want to disappoint him.

He draws his hand out of my panties. It's back on my shoulder, and I kneel. He arranges my hair again, over my shoulder to expose my back, pushing my head forward a little so I'm kneeling, head bowed, like a penitent seeking forgiveness before a god.

He kisses my shoulder again, pushes the dress a little farther down my arms, arranging me. Preparing me. And when he straightens and turns on the television to a random channel, the volume up, I know what he's going to do. I know exactly why he bought that cord. Why the old man looked at me like he did.

I know.

16

SEBASTIAN

She's beautiful.
Perfect.
Her skin is pristine, unmarked. Hair black, the darkest waterfall but for that rebellious, silver streak. Wild and defiant, like her.

All that perfection, all that unblemished skin, it makes me want to mark it up, brand my name on it, burn it into the back of her neck. Hear her scream. Know she's mine.

Even the bottoms of her small feet, their vulnerability as she kneels before me, toes curled under her, waiting for her punishment—my little penitent—even those feet make me want to mark. Brand. Own.

I swallow, pick up the coiled leather, wrap it around my fist once, twice. My dick is hard, and I'll fuck her when I'm finished. Fuck her from behind while I watch her face in the mirror. While I fill her up.

Sick bastard.

I smile at that voice.

Yes, I am.

"Don't turn around." I may want her tears, but I don't want to mark her pretty face.

She makes a small, nervous sound, gives a nod of understanding. She's looking down, not at me, not at us. Not when we're like this.

I move a little to the side and eye the broadest part of her shoulders. She trembles slightly while she waits. I wish I could slide a hand into her panties, feel if anticipation makes her as wet as it makes me hard. I should make her touch herself while I punish her. Maybe I will. But not yet. Pain first.

The sound of the first lash is the sweetest, the finest strand of perfect leather burning a line into her skin. Blemishing it. Interrupting all that perfect beauty.

But her gasp, it's sweeter still.

Her body rocks forward, and she catches herself, hands on the floor in front of her. The dress slides lower down her arms, to her waist, the cups of her bra at the tops of her hard nipples.

Her eyes meet mine in the mirror. I wonder what I look like to her. Huge as I stand over her, makeshift whip in my hand, cock hard as steel pressing against my pants, my body coiled tight.

The skin around her dark eyes is red from crying. Her mouth is a small O, but she can't be surprised.

I gesture for her to get back into position. She does, bowing her head slightly, hands small balls on her thighs, her body more tense than mine.

The second lash lines up perfectly beneath the first and this time, when her body jerks forward, she cries out, like the stroke pushed the air from her lungs.

I watch that line of red, thin and angry, striping even the backs of her arms, at the crease of her armpit.

I should make her raise her arms up, whip the underside.

Another time.

Another lash, and she's on her hands and knees.

"How many?" she pants. Sweat beads on her forehead.

"Back in position." I may do the bottoms of her feet yet.

"I wasn't going to go on the train," she tries again.

"This isn't about the train." It's not and it is. It's about everything. It's to punish her for disobeying, for taking the money I'd left behind, for failing my test, for proving me right.

But it's also about submission. It's about her being the Willow Girl. *My* Willow Girl.

My fist tightens around the cord. "Back in position. Now."

She wipes the back of her hand across her eyes and this time, when she's back in position, her hands are closed around her thighs, her knuckles white, shoulders tense. She squeezes her eyes shut when I ready my arm.

This stroke is harder. She lets out a scream, and I curse the fact that we're here in this hotel, that I have to have the television on. That I can't hear her scream break perfect silence.

I lash her again and again and again, until I count ten lines, not a single one crossing the other, each laid perfectly, neatly, obediently, beneath the last. Helena's leaning on one arm, half on her hands and knees, breathing hard, trying to keep her position, failing, yet too proud to beg for mercy.

I swallow, adjust the crotch of my pants. Her eyes follow the movement and rage fills them.

Fuck, but I like her like this.

"You're getting off on this," she accuses.

"Not yet, but I will."

"You're a dirty, sick bastard."

I snort. Talk about the pot calling the kettle black. She's as dirty as I am. "Put your hand inside your panties."

She searches my eyes, gives a panicked shake of her head.

"Do it. Put your hand inside your panties and rub your clit."

"No."

With one quick flick of my wrist, I lash the bottoms of her feet. She gasps and squeals at once and instinctively reaches back to cover them.

I crouch down, grip a handful of hair, tug. "I said put your hand inside your panties and rub your clit."

She does it slowly, neck craned at an awkward angle, eyes locked on mine. I watch her face, see her fingers work in my periphery.

"Are you wet?" I ask, fisting my hand in her hair.

"I hate you."

"But are you wet?" I lean closer, inhaling deeply. "Because I can smell you." I reach the whip hand into her panties, and from between her fingers, rub inside her folds. I smile. "You're as dirty as me, Helena," I say, dragging my hand out, an inch of the leather wet.

I stand back up.

Her eyes follow my movement in the mirror. She's still rubbing her pussy. I raise my arm and lay the lash across her back. She grunts, but rubs harder, her eyes on mine as I do it again and again and again.

Until the whole of her back is marked.

Perfect in a different way now.

Until I can't stand it anymore and I grip her arm, the one that's rubbing her pussy, and raise her to her feet.

She keeps rubbing, and I know she's close. I should whip her to orgasm, but I can't wait. I press her to the mirror, her breath fogging it instantly, and shove her panties down. She's still rubbing, and the wet sounds of her pussy make me harder.

I push my pants and briefs down and lift her dress and bend my knees to get under her, the leather still coiled around my fist when I lift her off her feet and impale her on my cock.

She slaps both hands, one wet, onto the mirror as I fuck her, both of us panting, breath damp and hot, her cunt dripping, greedy around me, sucking me up, squeezing me hard.

Within moments, she's coming and then I'm coming. My mouth is pressed against the side of her face. I can hear her breathe, hear her come, and fuck I want to fill her up and keep her full of me, put my seed inside her, make her hold it there, keep a piece of me inside her because with her, I can't ever get enough.

I can't ever get close enough.

Deep enough.

I hold her to me as I slide out, take two steps back, and we sit on the floor. We're out of breath. She's cradled between my knees, and I push hers open. We watch our combined cum leak out of her pussy, the sound of the TV—an infomercial selling a miracle face cream—finally coming into focus as our breathing settles.

She looks at me over her shoulder, and hate is inside her eyes. Hate and rage.

I like her like this. I like her angry. Feral. And when she spins and lunges at me, her hands claws, like a cat, I grab her wrists and laugh and topple onto my back. She's on top of me, and we're a half-dressed, sloppy mess.

She's battling me. I think if I let her go, she'll claw my eyes out.

"Not like this," I say, flipping us over so her back is on the rug. I know it burns. I know the fresh stripes on her back burn like hell, and I push her down into the rough carpet. "A notch," I say.

She stops. I let her up a little, let her go, and she leans against the bed, legs still wide, knees up so I can see her cunt, the dress a rag held to her waist by two buttons.

"You said no notches. Not here."

"But you said you didn't want that. And then you proved it. You want it rough. You don't want me nice."

"You're not nice," she says.

"No, you're right, I'm not. And now, I get a notch."

She swallows. I stand, go into the other room where my cell phone is in my jacket pocket, and dial the front desk. I order a bottle of champagne and a paring knife. I know they think I'm crazy, but when I'm spending this kind of money, I could give a fuck.

I hang up. She's standing in the doorway, nearly naked from the waist up, her hair a mess, cum sliding down her thigh and over the inside of her knee. I give her a grin. Fuck. She's beautiful like this. Fucking crazy. Feral.

That's the word. Like a cat. A wild, feral cat.

I take her into the bathroom. She doesn't fight me when I strip off her clothes and mine and run the shower—cool because I'm considerate of her fresh wounds—and we step inside. I wash her and kiss her and want to fuck her again.

When we're out and dried off, I walk into the living room where the champagne and the paring knife have been delivered. She follows me. We're both naked. I pop the cork on the champagne and pour two flutes but leave them on the tray and pick up the knife.

She backs up a step.

I take hold of her, pull her to me, look down over her naked body, and hold out the handle of the knife to her.

She looks at it, cautiously looks at me.

"My notch," I say, holding out my arm, the one scarred by the last notch.

She takes the knife, eyes still narrowed like she's expecting me to pounce, to turn the tables.

Holding her wrist, I guide her hand to me. "Carve it out."

"You're sick."

"Do it."

She shakes her head no.

"Do it, Willow Girl," I say through gritted teeth. "And make it hurt."

17

HELENA

A hint of red comes through the gauze on the inside of his arm. I look at it as he puts on a dress shirt.

He had to make me do it. I couldn't. Like the last time when I held my pocketknife to his belly and couldn't do it. He looks at me as he slides the cuff links through the slits at his cuffs. Raw, unpolished diamonds, the color of charcoal. Like his eyes.

I'm still naked, holding a flute of champagne, not having taken a sip. He pours his second glass. "Don't you like champagne?"

"It's for celebrations. We're not celebrating anything."

"Sure we are. You and me, Helena. We're celebrating the fact that we understand each other."

"What are you talking about?"

"Isn't it obvious? Our sexual compatibility—"

I snort.

He grins.

"Sweetheart, when I fuck you sweet, your orgasm is a fucking murmur. But when I fuck you hard, when I whip you, fuck. Your cunt swallows up my cock like it can't get enough."

I feel my face burn and can't hold his gaze. "I don't."

He chuckles, takes my jaw in his hand, and makes me look at him.

"You like it rough. Big fucking deal."

He lets me go and walks over to the dresser to pick up the other cuff link. He's wearing a tux. Right now, with his shirt hanging open, I can see the cut of every muscle on his abs and chest. I can't stop looking.

My dress is hanging in a garment bag he had delivered sometime this afternoon while I was out, but he won't let me see it yet. He also won't tell me where we're going.

"You never told me how you found me this afternoon," I say, taking a sip. I don't know if I like champagne or not. It's my first time drinking it, and it does go down smooth.

"I had a man on you."

"What?"

"It's not a big deal. I couldn't bring you with me to my meeting, and the alternative was leaving you on the island with my family. Would you have preferred that?"

"No. But you had someone watching me? Did you plant the money too?"

He doesn't reply to that but puts the cuff link on the other sleeve then buttons his shirt bottom to top before tucking it into his pants.

"Sebastian?"

"Drop it, Helena. It's done."

"But—"

"Drop it."

I do because he's right, it's done. And I can't be surprised he did it.

Sebastian briefly disappears into the bathroom, returns with a bottle of lotion, and sits on the edge of one of the chairs. "Come here." His knees are wide, and he's pointing between them.

I drink the rest of my champagne and go to him, sit on the floor between his legs with my back to him.

Like earlier, he lifts my hair off my back. I should hate this. I should be repulsed by him, by his touch, but I crave it. Crave his hands on me. And it's not just sexual. I like him taking care of me. He can be so gentle, more tender than anything I've ever felt before.

I remember what he said about cocooning me when I sleep, but at that moment, he touches a line on my back, I wince, remember what he did just an hour ago. It should harden me.

"Do you always have to hurt to get off? I mean, with other girls too." Wow. Do I want to know?

He doesn't answer right away. He's rubbing lotion onto my back, massaging it in, and it feels good.

"I like rough sex. Like you do."

"This is different than rough sex."

He considers, and I wait, his hands moving back and forth so tenderly, I want to moan.

"I want *you* like this," he says, his voice level.

I glance back. He's watching me, no mocking look, no smile. Something else. Something deeper. Darker.

"Why?"

He shakes his head. "I just do."

"Is it because I'm the Willow Girl?"

That was the wrong thing to say. His face shuts down, and he gets up. "Fuck the Willow Girl."

He goes to the garment bag and unzips it. I get to my feet. Inside is a floor-length evening gown in a deep purple satin draped beautifully on the velvet hanger. I can almost feel how that material will glide over me, move with me, like I'm wearing nothing.

"This is the color of your eyes when you're about to come. Almost black, but not quite. Like the edge of midnight." He touches the gemstone belt. "The stars inside."

I look at him. "You say the strangest things sometimes, Sebastian."

Like he sees everything. Like he thinks in poetry. Like he feels...something he can't feel. I clear my throat and turn to the shoe box. I couldn't care less about what's inside or how beautiful the dress is. I just can't have him keep looking at me like he is.

He picks up the box, opens it. Inside is a pair of high-heeled gemstone sandals to match the belt of the dress. I reach out to gingerly touch them.

"They don't bite."

I give him a sideways glance, wonder at the cost of everything, wonder why he did it. I pick up the shoes and try them on. They're so uncomfortable but so beautiful, I don't even care. I've never worn anything like this.

When I look up, I see how he's looking at me.

"I should get dressed."

He nods, takes the dress off the hanger, unzips the tiny zipper low on the back.

"People will see my back."

"Let them. Let them want what we have."

What we have. What do we have?

He slips the dress over my head, and I turn my back to him to zip it. I look at myself in the mirror, wonder how it's such a perfect fit.

The two upside-down triangles of cloth leave as much of my breasts exposed as they cover. The high empire waist makes me look taller than I am, and I realize the dress is split from the ankle all the way up to the waist. The back has slightly more material, so the split isn't as obvious. I pull the two sides apart and can see right up to my navel. I turn to him.

"I can't wear this out."

He draws my hands away and the dress drops and covers me to almost midthigh.

"Only I'll see," he says.

His eyes are darker, and when he looks at me like that, I want him again.

He checks his watch. "Ready?"

"Where are we going?"

"Dinner and the opera."

"Opera?" I can't help but smile.

"Faust. I hope you'll like it."

"A man sells his soul to the devil for love."

"You know it?"

"I've just read the book. I've never been to an opera." I feel suddenly very Midwestern.

"We'll have to drop in at a friend's party between dinner and the opera."

"A party?"

"Drinks, really." He opens the door.

"Oh." I try to seem more confident than I feel. "Okay."

He slides his hand under my hair and caresses my back lightly, like he likes to feel the welts he left or something. We ride down on the elevator. This time, we don't take a taxi. The driver of a waiting sedan opens the back door when he sees us, and I climb in with Sebastian close behind.

Nighttime Verona is very different to how it looked earlier today. For one thing, I feel a little more at ease. How that makes any sense is crazy, but I glance over at Sebastian, who is listening to a message on his phone. That's just how I feel. Like I'm not alone out there and uncertain and lost.

That's how I felt this afternoon, I guess. And I'm very aware that tomorrow, we'll go back to that island, to his horrible family, but I can't think about that, not that or what it means for me. Not tomorrow or the day after or the years after.

Dinner is more relaxed than I expected it to be. As fancy as we look, Sebastian takes me to a small pizza place just outside of town.

"This is my favorite place to eat when I come here. I hope you don't mind."

"Why would I mind?"

"That it's not a nicer restaurant."

I look around at the brightly lit place, at the man standing in the kitchen which is visible over the counter, at the people in jeans and T-shirts eating pizza.

"This is actually exactly my kind of place," I say, smiling.

Sebastian walks me into the kitchen where the man rolling out dough stops to hug him, surprised at seeing him. He gives me a wink and says something to Sebastian that I don't understand. This is probably the most relaxed I have ever seen Sebastian as he pats the old man's back and laughs loudly.

We go out back, and I am surprised to find a small plastic table with two plastic chairs set along the river. Lanterns hang overhead, and it's all very romantic.

Or it would be if it weren't us.

We sit on the rickety chairs and within a few minutes, we're eating thin slices of pizza more delicious than any I've ever tasted.

"You like it?" Sebastian asks me.

"I'm on my third slice, so yeah, I like it."

He nods, drinks from the can of grape soda.

I chuckle.

"What?" he asks.

"I don't picture you as a grape soda kind of guy."

"You don't know me yet."

Yet. "I guess not."

When we're done, we say good-bye and thank the owners.

Twenty minutes later, we pull through the tall gates of an old mansion where soft yellow lights illuminate the large double doors of the entrance. Two men in uniforms open them for us. I can hear the soft sound of a piano from outside as well as the tinkling of glasses, the murmur of conversation.

I don't need to see the elegantly dressed men and

women who turn in our direction when we enter to know I don't belong here.

The women are dressed like I am, but differently. They wear their dresses where suddenly, I feel like mine wears me, if that makes any sense. Their hair is elegantly done, and I'm sure I'm the only woman here who isn't wearing any makeup. I think how much more I liked the rickety-old chairs at the pizza place.

But one look at Sebastian tells me how comfortable he is in this company. How at home.

An older couple come toward us, smiling at Sebastian. With them is a girl who's maybe a couple of years older than me or my age but a hundred times more elegant. The women cast a glance at me, do a quick once-over, and turn their attention to Sebastian. The younger one's gaze hovers maybe a moment longer, and I'm immediately on my guard. She's prettier than me, without a doubt, with her dark hair in an elegant twist, false lashes accentuating her soft green eyes, and breasts jutting out, seeming as if they want to tear through the fine material of her white Grecian goddess dress.

And to top it off, they speak in Italian. At once, all three turn to me, and I hear my name.

"Helena, this is Mr. Vitelli, his wife Alexa, and their daughter, Alexa."

They share the same name? Maybe that's an Italian tradition? Whatever it is, I decide I don't like them. Especially the younger Alexa, whose dark nipples are almost poking a hole through her dress.

"Pleasure to meet you," Mr. Vitelli says. "I hope you're enjoying our lovely city."

"I am, thank you. It's beautiful." I notice the two women only give me half a smile.

A waiter comes with a tray of champagne. Everyone takes a glass, and we're led deeper into the room. I awkwardly stand at Sebastian's side while they continue their conversation.

The younger Alexa laughs at something Sebastian says and touches his shoulder flirtatiously. I raise an eyebrow and finish my drink. In the next room, I spy a long dining table loaded with food.

"Excuse me."

Before Sebastian can refuse, I slip away and walk toward it, swapping out my empty glass with a full one from a passing waiter. I find a place where I can watch them. I notice Sebastian's eyes on me even as he speaks to the Vitelli family.

Although I'm not hungry, I pick up a piece of bruschetta and bite into it, not caring that the people near me turn to look at the loud crunch, and work my way around the table before I find Sebastian standing beside me.

I face him and stuff a fat olive into my mouth.

"Where do you put all the food?" he asks. I did eat six slices of pizza, but in my defense, they had a thin crust, and I hadn't eaten all day.

I shrug a shoulder.

"Okay?" he asks.

"It's not my kind of crowd."

"Ah." He looks around, slides a hand around the back of my neck, holding me there, his thumb rubbing one of the welts. "Well, we don't have to stay long. It'll be over before you know it."

"It's okay. I'm fine. Go talk to your friends." *With their see-through dresses and pointy nipples.*

Sebastian turns to me, studies me, situates us so he's blocking me from view. He cups the back of my head in one hand and slides his other hand between the layers of my dress and cups my sex.

I gasp.

He leans in close. "You and me, we have a secret. Lots of secrets between us. These people, they're an obligation. You're what I want."

I look into his eyes, and it feels like the island is so far away, so long ago. It feels like we've been here forever, and it feels like he means what he says.

I nod, but I'm not really sure why.

He drags his hand away. The dress drapes back into place, the satin soft against my naked skin.

"I need to go talk to Vitelli for a few minutes. Some family business. We'll leave after. You going to be okay if I leave you here? No treks to the train station?"

"No treks anywhere in these shoes. I'm a big girl. I'll be fine."

He nods and walks off in the direction I see Mr. Vitelli waiting, looking more serious than he had a little bit ago as he leads him into a room off one of the three hallways.

I spend a few minutes holding up a wall before deciding to hunt for a telephone, but I find only locked doors. Nowhere to slip inside and make a phone call unnoticed. I'd love to talk to Amy, even for a few minutes.

When I find a bathroom, I go inside and lock the door. It's a luxurious space large enough for a velvet couch, the counter littered with expensive perfumes and soaps. I take my time and when I'm finished, I find three women have gathered to use it.

I slip past and hope to find Sebastian ready to go, but when I don't see him in the main room, I walk toward the stairs where couches have been set up and people who want a little more privacy have converged.

I climb up and from there, I can see the whole of the first floor. I'm looking at the hallway where Sebastian went. When I see a door open and the Grecian goddess emerge adjusting her dress, I'm curious. But what I don't expect is Sebastian to follow a moment later, eyes hard, looking around the room.

He wipes something from the corner of his mouth, and when he looks up toward the balcony, I shrink back, slip into the shadows. I don't go downstairs for a full ten minutes, and I don't know why I can't shake that feeling that I've been betrayed.

I haven't.

All I am is his Willow Girl.

His Willow Whipping Girl.

How much more obvious do I need it to be?

18

SEBASTIAN

Helena is sitting stiffly beside me in the second row of the opera. I have my hand at her thigh, but she's keeping her legs tightly closed and gripping the edges of her chair. She hasn't looked at me once since it began. She barely did on the drive over.

Although, I was distracted when we left. Vitelli knows who Helena is. Knows about the Willow Girl. He shouldn't, but my dear stepmother had been to visit him. I assume this is where she and Ethan had come to on one of their nights off the island.

I'm not the only one who's broken the rules of the Willow game. Secrecy is an important one. But there are others and I knew the moment I chose Helena, that slash of pig's blood on her sheath would haunt me.

I guess I'm not surprised Lucinda was here. She's

is preparing for war. So am I. And I'm better armed than she. This trip was fruitful, my guess correct.

But I know using what I learned against her will hurt Ethan, even if it does save Helena. At least from one brother. I'll worry about the other later, though. I have to think about how to handle Ethan. If I'm not careful, this will damage him, and I've done enough damage.

I glance at Helena, who sits stiff as a board beside me. Quite frankly, it's pissing me off. What I'm doing, I'm doing for her.

I lean in to her ear. "What the fuck is the problem?"

She gives me a lethal look.

The soprano hits a high note, and the music abruptly stops. After a moment of utter silence, the people around us stand and cheer. I take Helena by the arm, raise her to stand, and walk her toward the aisle before it's overrun during the intermission.

"What are you doing? It's not finished."

"We're going somewhere more private to watch the rest."

She glances up at me. "I'm fine where we are."

"I'm not."

Remarkably, I don't have to shove anyone out of my way as I maneuver us east of the stage and to a service door. I push it open, see the actors on their way to their dressing rooms, hear the staff hurrying to prepare for the Second Act.

"I don't think we're supposed to be here," she says, pulling back.

"Shh." I glance both ways, and we cross the hall and walk a little farther to get to another door. It's darker in here. I use the flashlight on my phone to guide us through the stored props.

She's slow because she's looking at everything.

We reach the curtained-off stairs. I push them aside and point. "This way."

She peeks up the narrow, stone staircase. "What's up there?"

"You'll see."

Her sense of adventure outweighs whatever it is she's upset about. She climbs the stairs, hands on either stone wall. At the top, there's another door. I reach over her to push it open. It sticks a little but eventually gives and a moment later, we're outside, in a small area that's a sort of balcony from where we can see the whole of the colosseum.

"Wow. Are we supposed to be here?" She looks down, up, at everything around her.

"No, probably not."

She turns to me. "How do you know about it?"

"My dad used to bring us here when we were little. We'd come to three operas a week some summers. It got a little dull, so Ethan, Gregory, and I would explore."

"They just let you explore? Here?"

"They didn't know exactly where we were."

The orchestra signals the Second Act is about to begin, and it seems to remind Helena of her annoyance. I see it on her face.

"What happened between dinner and this?"

She turns to me. "Nothing."

"Something."

She studies me, and I wait.

"What were you doing in that room with Alexa 2.0?"

I'm confused. Although the Alexa 2.0 is funny.

"Were you spying?"

"No. I was upstairs on the balcony. I saw her come out of a room, and you followed soon after. She was adjusting her dress like her boob fell out, which I wouldn't be surprised if it did, considering." She rolls her eyes and purposefully turns her gaze to the stage.

"You sound jealous, Helena."

She snorts. "You didn't have to take me to the party. You could have left me at the hotel."

"So you could run off to the train station again?"

She gives me a glare.

I get behind her, push her hair over her shoulder, and put my hands beside hers on the stone wall. I kiss her neck, the curve of her shoulder, the first welt on her back.

"Stop."

I slide one hand inside the triangle covering her breast and the other between her legs.

"Alexa 2.0 is like a piece of birthday cake."

I'm rubbing her pussy, kissing another line of red. She turns her head.

"What do you mean?"

"She's nice to look at. Maybe makes your mouth water."

She shoves at my forearm. "Then you should go have a slice."

"That's the point. Everyone can have a slice. Everyone has."

"Have you?"

"A long time ago." I pull my hand from her breast and make her look at me when she turns away. "And I don't want seconds." I kiss her. Her mouth opens, and her pussy is wet in my hand. "You're what I want. This mouth, this pussy. You."

The orchestra begins to play as Margarita comes on the stage, singing her woeful song.

Helena turns and puts her hands on the wall.

I draw her hips back, nudge her legs wide with my own, and the dress splits in two, exposing her to me.

I take a minute, stand back and admire her, pull her hips farther so she's bent over, and I look at her like this, waiting for me, open for me. I want her. I want her like I've never wanted anything else in my life.

One hand on her hip, I hold her open as I undo my belt, unzip my pants, shove them and my briefs down. I slide into her pussy as I push her long hair off her back.

The raised lines beneath my fingers makes me harder. I close my hand around the back of her neck and hold her with one hand while with the other, I keep her ass spread open so I can see her, watch her pussy stretch to take me, see the tiny ring of her asshole.

I want all of her, her pussy, her ass, her mouth. I want to fill every hole at once.

She arches her back as I thrust into her, and the sounds of our fucking, of wet pussy swallowing up hard cock, of moans and groans and skin slapping against skin rival that of the soprano. When she fists her hands and I feel her squeeze me, throb around me, I come too, filling her up, squeezing the back of her neck, digging my fingers into her hip.

More bruises, my marks on her, only mine.

When I pull out, I watch cum drip out of her, drip onto the floor. I turn her to me and kiss her mouth as she wraps her arms around my neck, fingers in my hair, nails digging into the skin of my scalp.

"You're mine, Helena," I say between kisses. "You're what I want."

19

HELENA

The drive back late the following afternoon is quiet. The sun is shining bright, so opposite the sheets of rain the day before.

I feel him glance at me, and I wonder what he sees. I wonder if things will change now.

I touch the ring on my finger, turn it a little, so the skull face is staring at me.

"What is that ring?"

He pays attention to everything. "My aunt gave it to me after the reaping." I can't help the accusatory tone in that last word.

"My Aunt Helena."

He nods, looks straight ahead.

"Did you decide if I can call her?"

He won't look at me when he replies. "Let's talk about it later."

"This is later, Sebastian."

Nothing.

"She gave it to me to remind me that not every Willow Girl dies," I say, unable to help myself. Unable to help that familiar darkness from creeping into my words.

We're nearing the docks. We'll be back on the island soon.

"I miss her."

"She lived with you, right?"

"Yes. I'd sometimes catch her and my mom in these top-secret meetings. I called them that because they were so strange about it. I realize now my aunt must have known about the money that would change hands when the next one of us was claimed."

By the time that day came, I felt like she hated my mother. I didn't know why, not then.

"I overheard them once. It was on our sixteenth birthday. I'd gone to my aunt's room to call her down for the celebration. She was out of her chair. She could walk, but she was so old, it was easier for her in the chair. But she was up on her feet, and my mom was sitting on the edge of her bed. They were arguing more loudly than usual, and my aunt did something I'd never expect from her. She slapped my mother's face, and I can still remember the sound of it and her exact words: *"You saw what they did to your sister and you'll put your babies on those blocks? And for what? You make me sick."*

There's more that I don't tell him. How my aunt

had told my mom it should have been her. That Libby wouldn't have done this. She would have chosen differently.

They had argued then, and my mom forbade her from coming to the birthday celebration. She locked her in her room like she was a child.

When I took Aunt Helena a piece of birthday cake later, she lied to me, told me she hadn't felt well enough to come. I think it was the only time she lied to me.

I take a long breath in. "Please let me call her today." I'm not above begging, not anymore. "You can be in the room. What are you afraid I'll say? I just want to talk to her, tell her I'm okay. Hear her voice."

What would my aunt think if I told her the truth? That I was starting to have feelings for my Scafoni master. Would she slap my face too?

He pulls into the parking lot, drives up to the docks. I recognize the man who greets us. He's the same one as yesterday.

Sebastian gets out, hands over the keys. He opens the trunk and takes out our overnight bag. When he opens my door, I just look up at him.

I can't get out. I don't want to. I feel my eyes filling up again because I'm scared and I don't want to go back, and it's worse now than before.

He sighs, tells the man to load the bag onto the

boat, and crouches down. He takes one of my hands into both of his.

"I don't want to go back there," I say.

"We have to, Helena."

I shake my head. "Why? You can decide. It's up to you what happens to me."

Not for long, though. Not for long.

My stomach turns at the thought.

"Listen to me, Helena."

I shake my head.

"Listen. My meeting in Verona, it was good news. I'm trying—" he stops abruptly, breathes in, changes track. "You have to trust me now. What I said to you yesterday, they weren't empty words."

I stop.

"I have no intention of passing you on to my brothers," he says.

"What? How? How can you stop it?"

He straightens so I have to look up at him and squint against the sun behind him.

"I can't tell you that. Just let me handle this my way and trust me. No one will touch you. You'll be safe."

"How can I be safe on that island? With them?"

His forehead is creased. He reaches down, unbuckles my seat belt, and lifts me out of the car.

"Give me a few days, and we'll talk again. Can you do that?"

"I don't have a choice, Sebastian."

No one is around when we get back. Apart from the bustle of food being prepared in the kitchen and the gardeners working outside, it's quiet. Sebastian has to make calls and disappears into his study. After spending an hour in my room, I decide to go outside, go for a walk.

The waning light lends a comforting backdrop to my walk. There won't be a single cloud in the sky tonight.

I walk past the swimming pool, the filter buzzing quietly, and step onto the grass, turn toward the small farm. It's just far enough from the house that the smell doesn't reach it.

A dozen chickens roam free and half that number of lambs. I wonder if they slaughter them. I guess they do. Why else keep lambs? Chickens for eggs maybe, but not all of them.

I pet the two lambs grazing by the fence as I pass and walk toward the vegetable garden, weaving through the neat rows of greens. When I see the strawberry patch in the farthest corner, I bend to pick a handful of ripe ones and plop them into my mouth one after another. They're smaller than the ones we get at home from the supermarket. Softer too, and a hundred times sweeter.

When I've had my fill, I wipe off my hands and turn to go back to the house. But I pause.

There's an unkept path between the trees here, and it leads to the east side of the island. I can take the long way back to the house.

Before I can talk myself out of it, I begin to walk steadily away from the house in the direction I'm not to go. One of the places forbidden to me. I'm curious why it's forbidden.

It's a longer walk than I realize, but that's partly the route I take. It's overgrown, if it was ever maintained to begin with, and becomes more of a hike. Flip-flops aren't the right footwear, I find out.

The foliage seems to change here too. It becomes wilder, rougher. The long branches of low bushes scratch at my legs as I walk, and I wish I'd brought a sweater. It's cooled down a lot since the sun set.

Just when I think I should turn back the trees give way to a clearing.

I stop at the edge of the large circle of hay-like grass and look at it, the Scafoni family mausoleum.

A chilly wind blows my skirt up and steals my breath as I stand taking it in, the gray stone building older than any other on the island, large and imposing and final.

I take a step into the clearing, and it's like I've stepped out of one world and into another. It's the strangest, creepiest feeling. I hug my arms to myself, rub them, tell myself to grow up. Of course, it's creepy. It's full of dead bodies or ashes or dust. But the key word is dead.

These Scafoni can't hurt me.

I force myself to walk toward the two wide stairs that lead to the large iron doors. They're more like garden gates than doors.

When I'm closer, I realize carved in the stone over the door is the body of an angel, androgynous, one of the wings clipped by time, the other grand. He or she kneels, hands on the ground, fingers curled but soft, head bowed, giving the impression of one who is broken or grieving. One who has accepted what has come to pass.

But then, when I get closer, I can see that beneath the thick strand of stone hair, the angel's face is just visible enough, and one eye looks straight out at me. It's a Watcher, standing guard over the Scafoni remains, not passive at all, but fierce.

And she knows I don't belong here.

It almost makes me stop. Almost.

But I steel my spine and reach out to brush the tips of my fingers against the gritty iron of the gate. It's slightly a jar, not quite closed, and I push.

It's so quiet here that the creak sounds a hundred times louder than it is. If I'd thought it was chilly outside, it's doubly so inside. A hanging lantern shines a red light over the space, illuminating the room just enough to let me see. A breeze blows, and something tickles my toes, making me gasp and jump until I realize it's just a dead leaf blown out of its resting place by the wind.

All around me, Scafoni names are carved in stone, dates beneath them. Birth and death. Iron candle holders, like long fingers, protrude from beside each name. Some have stubs of candles, some are filled with dirt. I read some of the names, the oldest ones. Hundreds of years old.

When I come upon Anabelle's, I stop. I reach out and touch the engraving.

Hers is one of the forgotten graves. And beside her is her son, Giuseppe.

His last name is listed as Scafoni-Willow.

I'm surprised at it. Surprised they'd not banish the name from this final resting place of the Scafoni family because they can't want to remember us in death.

Although the Willow part of the name seems to be vandalized, like someone took a jagged stone and scratched it through a hundred times, but it's still there. Still among the Scafoni dead, hanging like a shadow over them even in death.

I reach out to touch it, trace the letters of my name.

Do I believe the story Sebastian told me about Anabelle? He could have lied. What's to prevent him from lying? Painting us in the worst possible light?

I drop my hand, cross to the newer stones. I find Joshua Scafoni's marker. Sebastian's father. The man who chose my Aunt Libby to be his Willow Girl. Beside it, I expect to find his mother, and I do see her, but there's one name between them. Timothy Scafoni.

Confused, I read the date. The child lived three days. I do the math. Do it again. It can't be.

"You shouldn't be here."

The voice makes me jump and I spin around, clutching my heart.

They sound so much alike, Gregory and Sebastian. You'd almost mistake the one for the other.

Not me, though. Gregory's voice carries a hint of malice in it. It's just a hint, but I hear it.

"You don't belong here, Willow Girl."

I swallow. I'd step back, but I'm already backed up against the stone grave wall, and the iron candle holders are digging into my back.

He takes a step toward me, looks just beyond me, comes close enough to touch me. But he doesn't.

"I got lost."

I can't move when he turns to me, when he's so close I can feel the heat of his body and all I see are his eyes and the way they watched me that night.

"I don't believe that," he says, his voice quiet. Almost gentle. Not quite, though. It's missing something to be gentle.

I wonder why he's wearing a suit and remember how, before he took me down from the whipping post, he took off his jacket and wrapped it around my shoulders. A small kindness.

I meet his eyes, but I can't read him.

"I'll go," I say.

"Did you do the math?" he asks, reaching for a candle and taking a lighter out of his pocket to light it.

My legs seem finally able to function again. I take a step away and watch him drip wax onto the stub of a candle in the holder at his father's marker, then push his candle into it, uniting the two.

He turns to me. "Did you?"

"Yes."

"Sebastian's not firstborn."

"Twins."

Gregory nods. "Timothy was first. Only survived days, though." He glances at Sebastian's mother's marker. "Killed her too, two years later."

"What do you mean?"

"Sebastian didn't tell you?"

I shake my head.

"His mother committed suicide. In here."

I glance at the marker, read the date of her death, the month, the day. It's the day her sons were born, just two years later. She killed herself on Sebastian's birthday.

Gregory steps toward me and again, I'm locked in place. Trapped.

"Still not scared of me?"

I shake my head quickly. Too quickly.

"What do you think he'll do when you learns you were in here?"

"Are you going to tell him?"

"I don't know." He slides his gaze over me. I'm wearing a T-shirt to cover the marks on my back, and a skirt. His eyes settle at my thighs for a minute, then a little higher. When he returns his gaze to mine, he cocks his head to the side. "He'll be mad. Pissed enough to use the whipping post for what it's meant for."

I swallow.

Gregory suddenly smiles, and his whole expression changes. It's disarming.

And calculated.

"The fact that he's not technically firstborn means he's not really head of the family. That role goes to the son who takes it."

"What do you mean?"

"I could want my own Willow Girl. Seems like fun."

"You're sick, you know that? Perverted"

"Maybe. Probably," he adds, as if agreeing after a moment's thought. "Still." He reaches out to touch my face, and I bat his hand away. "I liked watching you come."

I swallow, feel sweat pool under my arms.

"Maybe you like sick and perverted. I mean, you seem to like my brother."

"Tell him if that's what you want. He won't do what you say."

"No? How well do you think you know my brother?" He pauses for effect. "You willing to risk it?"

I study his eyes, try to read what he's thinking.

"I'll tell you what. I'll keep your secret. This way, you and I, we can have our own." He places his fingers on my jaw, and for a minute, I wonder if he's measuring the fingertips against the fading bruises. "Just between us."

He's fucking with me.

I pull away, force my legs to move. I get to the door before I turn around.

"I'd rather you tell him," I say. "I'd rather take a whipping than keep a secret with you."

It's full dark when I run back to the house. I don't stop once, not even when I lose one of my flip-flops. I go straight upstairs, up to my room, slam the door behind me.

I'm in such a panic, I don't even notice Lucinda, not until I've trapped myself inside with her. She's reclining on my bed, her feet crossed at the ankles, her dirty shoes on my comforter.

She's holding a torn envelope, reading the sheet of paper. I think I recognize the handwriting, but she moves it too quickly for me to be sure and sits up.

"What the hell are you doing in here?" I ask.

She slides her legs off the bed, stands, and looks me over. I look down too, at my one bare foot, at the scratches along my legs and the dirt on my feet.

"I hope you didn't track dirt into the house."

She walks across to the window and pushes it open to glance outside.

"What do you want?" I ask.

She turns back to me, sets whatever she was reading on the dresser, and gives me a grin. "Have a good trip? A romantic little getaway?"

"Yes, actually. It was refreshing being away from you."

"Well, aren't we lucky to have you back."

"What are you doing in here?"

Lucinda shrugs a shoulder, pulls open one of the drawers, and rummages through it. She picks out a pair of panties, a tiny pair, and holds it on her long red fingernail.

"Does he like you in this? Likes you to whore it up?"

I go to her, take the panties, and drop them into the drawer before shoving it shut.

"You have no right to be in here. Get out."

"It's my house. I can be anywhere I want." She goes to the closet, turns on the light, but stays in the doorway to peek in, then looks back at me. "Libby whored it up too. Joshua loved that."

I don't want to hear this. As hungry as I am about my Aunt Libby's time here, I don't want to hear it from her.

"You know, Sebastian should share you," she says, coming back into the bedroom and sitting down on the chaise like this was her room. "Joshua shared Libby. She took all three at once. One in her mouth, one in her ass and the other in her dirty cunt." Her lip curls, and the word sounds more vulgar on her lips than it even is.

"She didn't have a choice," I say.

She smiles a cold, cruel smile. "She came like a whore. She was loud, louder than you are. Or don't you come? Doesn't my son make you come?"

"He's not your son."

She seems surprised I know that. "Did he tell you that? Fascinating."

"What's fascinating about that?"

"Since he's feeding you piecemeal, I'm just surprised he chose that little tidbit. Although Sebastian's always been clever. Too clever. I suppose it would endear you to him to know my weak sister, his mother, hanged herself."

I hear hatred in her words, the tone of her voice, and it's directed toward her dead sister.

"What's wrong with you? She lost a son."

"Oh? How do you know that?"

I don't answer, not right away. "Sebastian told me."

"Really? He doesn't tell anyone that. Not even his Willow Girl. Even if he is smitten. You're a sneaky whore."

I don't reply.

"My husband was smitten too. Truth be told, he loved his Willow whore. She was meeker than you.

More obedient. Although maybe that has to do with my strict regimen of discipline. Kept her in line."

"You beat her."

"Disciplined her. There's a difference."

"Call it what you want."

"I saw that girl with her mouth stuffed full of my husband's cock more than without it."

She's looking away like she's reminiscing, like it's a fond memory.

"He'd make me prepare her for him. Make me shave her pussy the way he liked. Wash her. Make me watch him fuck her. But in exchange, I disciplined her as I saw fit."

"Why are you telling me this?"

She shrugs a shoulder. "Boredom."

"Were you jealous of my aunt? Is that why you hate us?"

She studies me, calculating her cruelty, measuring the destruction of her words.

"Maybe. Maybe I was jealous of his affection for her. The tenderness he showed her after her sessions with me. But not jealous that he'd rather fuck her than me. I don't need a man. I never have."

"Yet you live with three of them, and from what I see, Sebastian rules."

Any suggestion of a smile vanishes. She gets up, comes toward me, stands inches from me.

"Did you know he didn't have to do this? Didn't have to take a Willow Girl?"

I set my jaw, hold her gaze.

She's a liar. I know that.

"He chose this. He can stop it at any time even. It's his right. Yet he chooses not to. He chooses to keep you here under his thumb. Chooses to continue the tradition of passing you down from one brother to the next to the next. He chooses this for you."

"I don't believe you." It's not true. It's not. He has no choice. If he didn't do it, Ethan would get his turn.

"I don't care what you believe. Truth is still truth. And it all just comes down to one thing. Money. He releases you from your obligation, and he forfeits his place as head of the Scafoni family. He loses everything. Sad little world we live in, isn't it, when money is worth more than a human life?"

She sets her long fingernail under my chin and raises it a little. We're eye to eye.

"I don't believe you."

"Believe what you want, Willow Girl. I'm actually here to give you a letter that came earlier." She gestures to the dresser where she'd dropped what she was reading when I came inside. "Got here two days after your arrival. Must have slipped Sebastian's mind to deliver it."

I see victory in her eyes, and I think about our notches, Sebastian and me. I think Lucinda would win this one. I know it before I even see what's inside the letter.

I walk away from her, pick up the letter and envelope. It's addressed to me, and I recognize the handwriting. It's from my sister, Amy.

I check the postmark, and she's right. It arrived when she said it did.

My heart races. I know it's bad news. I know it before I turn it over to read it.

"Luckily, I found it in his trash can and fished it out. I thought you should have it."

I open the sheet, see the few lines of Amy's note. Watch the newspaper clipping fall to the floor.

"There's a boat waiting for you. Remy will take you to the airport. Flight leaves in two hours. You get one chance to get out of here, Willow Girl. Don't fuck it up, and don't let anyone see you." She digs into her pocket. A moment later, she sets a passport, I assume mine, on the table by the door.

"Why would you help me?"

"I'm not helping you. I'm helping myself."

She then walks out, and her words trickle in slowly as I read Amy's note. And as I bend to pick up the clipping, a tear blots the ink.

20

SEBASTIAN

"You need to watch your girl," Gregory says as he takes a seat across from me in my office. "She's going to get herself into trouble."

"Saw the marks you left on her wrist."

"She bruises easily. What's the vitamin that's missing if you bruise easily? Maybe it's because she doesn't eat meat."

"Don't be a dick, Greg."

He scratches the back of his neck. "I want a piece, Sebastian."

"No."

"Why not? It won't be the first time we shared a girl. Hell, you practically offered her the other night."

"I said no." I move my hands onto my lap, feel them fist. I can't read what he's thinking. My younger brother is too good at masking his thoughts. I know growing up he had to be, but it's not how we are, he and I.

"What's changed?" he asks.

"I'm keeping her, Gregory. That's what's changed."

He studies me for a long time, then nods. Gets up. Without a word on what I just said, he walks out of my office. I watch him go, and I know it's not going to be this easy. No fucking way, not with him.

I get up and head upstairs to Lucinda's room. I knock. A moment later, I hear her call to enter. I do.

She's sitting at her desk, her back to it. I close the door behind me and go inside, sit on the sofa across from her. I look around her room. She's got the second biggest one, second only to mine. I moved her out of the master once I took control of the family. Lucinda and I, we have a long and ugly history.

"Sebastian," she says, getting up and pouring two whiskeys from the bottle on the corner of her desk. She hands me one. "You never visit me here."

"I want to talk in private."

"Can't imagine what about." She settles back into her seat and takes a long swallow of her drink.

"I know, Lucinda."

She cocks her head to the side, and that grin, that victorious smirk, I want to wipe it from her face.

"What do you know, Sebastian?" she asks, raising her drawn-in eyebrows high.

"I know about Ethan."

For a millisecond, there's a flicker of panic on her face, just for the tiniest fraction of time. If I didn't know her so well, I would have missed it.

"I don't want to hurt him—"

"Late for that, isn't it?" she interrupts.

"That's why I'm here to talk to you." I ignore her jab, push through.

"I don't know what you're talking about."

"You going to make me say it?" I ask.

She stares back at me, her face stone. She sips from her drink, clears her throat, remains silent.

"Fine. I'll say it. I don't know who his father is, and I don't care, but he doesn't have a drop of Scafoni blood in him."

Stone turns to ice.

"He has no right to any Scafoni inheritance. None of it. Not a penny," I continue. I want her to be crystal clear.

Her face is red when she finally speaks. "And after what you did, it will kill him to find out he's not your brother."

I break eye contact, because she's right. I swallow what's in my glass, stand, walk across to where she's sitting to refill it. I don't look at her when I say this next part.

"That's why I'm here. You're his mother. You can't want that for your son."

I take my time returning to my place on the sofa, and when I sit back down, I see she's thinking. Calculating. And I'm not sure at all she'd put Ethan's well-being above her own.

"This is about the girl. The Willow whore with the pig's blood on her sheath. You broke the rules, Sebastian. You were supposed to take a virgin."

She's right. I have one on her, she has one on me, and we can destroy everything for each other. In fact, the only person left standing if we did would be Gregory. And I feel a weight settle in my gut when I remember his eyes from just minutes ago. The way he acquiesced so easily. The way he walked out of my office, so accepting.

He's biding his time. He's going to let things play out because he knows how this will end. One way or another, he'll get his Willow Girl because even if I am able to diffuse the Ethan/Lucinda situation, Gregory has a right to her.

"I consider Ethan my brother, you know that," I say.

"Since when? Since the *accident*?" She puts that last word in air quotes.

"You never encouraged a relationship between us, not from day one."

"Oh boo-hoo." She stands, turns to refill her

glass. "You need inner-child therapy, Sebastian? Go tell someone how horrible your mother was to you."

"You're not my mother. You never have been."

"Grow up."

"I did. I grew up fast under your cane."

"You were always a filthy boy. You needed the cane." She pauses, grits her teeth, lifts her chin and inhales a deep breath.

"Don't push me on this, Lucinda."

"What are you offering?"

"Ethan won't have Helena. He won't touch her. You take him off the island for a few months, take him somewhere he likes to go, tell him whatever you need to tell him to change his mind about the Willow Girl. When he's understood it, you'll both be welcomed back, and he will never know the truth about his parentage, and you'll keep your place here, your status. Your allowance." I wonder if this last one isn't all that matters to her.

She grins. "What about Gregory? Have you thought about what he wants? What he'll do once Ethan is out of the picture? You think he won't contest the fact that she's not a virgin? That you're not technically firstborn. That you broke the rules? He'll have you disinherited before you can profess your love to that whore."

"What the fuck do you know about love?" The huskiness in my voice surprises me.

"Hit a nerve, did I? You're so easy. As easy as your whore."

"What are you talking about, Lucinda?"

She ignores my question, goes to the window, and pushes the curtain aside with one long, bony finger, one corner of her mouth curving upward. She then turns to me.

"One time," she says, "I'll make the deal with you. Take Ethan off the island. Away from this place. But he gets to have her once. One time. You can even dictate which hole he fucks."

I'm on my feet, hands fisted at my sides. I stalk over to her. She backs up, but that look in her eyes, the one that screams victory, it mocks me, and I can't fucking stand it. Can't stand her. I close my hand around her throat and shove her against the wall.

"He doesn't lay a single finger on her. Not one."

She smiles, even as her eyes redden, bulge, my hand squeezing her scrawny neck.

"Your hate makes you ugly, Lucinda. Makes you old. An old, jealous bitch."

She's got her hands on my forearm now, is trying to drag me off. She's struggling for breath. I give one more squeeze before releasing her, watching her sputter and cough.

"You have twenty-four hours to decide before I tell Ethan he's a bastard."

"You're just like your father. You fell for that whore like he did his. You let your Willow Girl come between your family, just like he did. I'll smile when they carve out the name on your stone, right next to his. Next to your dead brother."

"You're a pathetic old woman," I say, walking out.

"Don't you dare walk out on me!"

I slam the door shut behind me, her words clawing at me, stalking me. Lucinda is a force to be reckoned with. This isn't over. I know that. It's not over by a long shot.

I go to Helena's room, knock once. It's more of a banging with my fist. "Helena. You in there?"

Nothing. I open the door, but the room's empty. I try the bathroom, knocking again, but finding it, too, empty. Using the connecting door, I go to my room. Maybe she went there. But she isn't here either.

"Helena?"

I hear the engine of the boat and rush to the window and I see Helena run toward it, watch her board. See the two figures on the boat.

"Helena!"

I turn, run for the door, but see the discarded letter on the floor. I bend to pick up the familiar note from her sister with her aunt's obituary inside.

Lucinda did this. Lucinda gave it to her.

I crush it in my hand and am about to get up when Lucinda reappears in the doorway.

"I told you not to fucking walk away from me." She stalks to me as I stand, and I hear the clicking before I see the gun she raises in her hand. Aims.

"What the fuck do you think you're doing?"

I see the rage on her face, and I charge toward her, almost reaching her before she pulls the trigger.

Almost.

A flash of light and a burning pain stuns me. I stumble once, twice, but somehow, I've got hold of her wrist and when I fall, she's falling too, and the gun goes off again and my shoulder burns.

I topple on top of her but a minute later, she shoves me off. I watch her rise to her feet, look down at me, and when I reach to touch my shoulder, warm liquid covers my hand.

"Lucinda," I start, trying to raise myself up through the pain, but something hits me on the back of my head. It feels like someone's slammed a brick against it.

I blink, try to force my eyes to stay open, but fall backward and all I feel is pain and all I see is black and all I hear is the sound of Lucinda's footsteps running out of the room and I'm left with my thoughts and they're churning, circling, exploding until they, too are fading.

Fading.

Gone.

21

HELENA

My Aunt Helena died the night I left.

She died while I was still on that plane.

She was dead when I asked him to let me call her over and over again, and he knew it and he didn't say a goddamned word.

Not one.

I didn't bother to pack anything. Nothing here is mine. I changed into a pair of jeans and grabbed a sweater, put on a pair of shoes, and picked up my passport. I walked out the door, and when I heard arguing coming from Lucinda's room, I ran. I scrambled down the stairs, out the front door, and outside, the night calm around me, the quiet sounds of crickets and soft waves same as the other nights. Like nothing outside has changed. Like everything is just the same.

Tonight, the lights guiding the path to the docks are off. I guess Lucinda took care of that. Of course, she did. She wants me off this island.

I stop for a moment, hesitate. Why? Why would she help me?

No, she's not helping me. She's helping herself. I have to give her one thing. She's been up front with me from day one. She's been awful, but honest. She hates me, but she doesn't play games with me. Not like Sebastian.

Does she see how close Sebastian is with me? Is that what it is? Am I threat to her? How? Why?

In my rush, I stumble over a stone raised a little higher than the others and fall down, scraping my knees. I look down at my hand, at the ring Aunt Helena gave me.

Aunt Helena is dead.

She died weeks ago, and Sebastian has known all this time.

Christ. I'm a fool. All that time in the car, me spilling my guts out about her. Telling him about that night, that secret I'd kept even from my sisters, I told him.

And when he told me to trust him, I did.

She said she found the letter in his trash can. Was he ever going to tell me? Or just avoid having to answer every time I asked him to let me make a call? Maybe work something out with my parents that they keep this a secret too.

If he's lied about this, what else is he lying about?

I didn't know about his twin brother. Never knew Sebastian isn't technically firstborn. That his place isn't cast in stone.

He told me about Lucinda being his stepmother, and I felt sorry for him. I felt sorry for him that his mother had died. If he'd told me she'd died on his birthday, he would have gotten even more sympathy out of me.

What else isn't he telling me? What else is there he's lying about?

Is it true what she said? That he didn't have to do this? That he could stop it at any time?

"And it all just comes down to one thing. Money. He releases you from your obligation, and he forfeits his place as head of the Scafoni family. He loses everything. Sad little world we live in, isn't it, when money is worth more than a human life?"

I get up, wince at the pain the tiny stones cut into my knees. The boat engine starts when I take my next step, and I wipe my face. I'm not crying over him. I'm not. My aunt is dead. These tears are for her.

I climb the steps up to the dock and go to the idling boat. Remy is at the steering wheel. He doesn't come to help me on. I climb on myself, but it's easy enough.

As soon as I'm on board, before I'm even seated, we pull away from the island.

I look back once, look back at the big, beautiful house with all its lights. With all its lies. All the liars inside it.

I hug my sweater to myself and move to step into the enclosed space of the boat, and I don't expect there to be anyone on the boat but me and Remy, but someone's inside the cabin. He stands as I enter. He's tall and big, but he's wearing a hoodie and I can't see his face.

Something tells me to turn, to get off the boat, but we're too far. When I try to run, a powerful hand closes around my arm, hurting me, bruising me.

I open my mouth to scream, but he smashes a cold, wet cloth over my face and just then, Remy turns around. But it's not Remy. It's Ethan. Ethan with a leering grin, watching me struggle, kick, and claw. And I realize my mistake too late.

Ethan's face is the last thing I see as the chloroform does its work, and I feel myself weaken, feel my body slump against the powerful chest of the man behind me, feel him let up a little as my arms drop to my sides and my knees give out.

I hit the hard deck of the boat, feel the engine vibrate as a boot shoves me rudely aside. The man makes his way out of the enclosed space, and I hear the muffled sound of speech, smell the smoke of a cigarette as I lose consciousness and we speed toward whatever destination Lucinda has planned for me.

I knew she wasn't doing this to help me.
But her intention wasn't ever to let me go.
It was only ever to take me from Sebastian.

* * *

*Thank you for reading **Taken**!*
I hope you love Sebastian and Helena.

*You can read the conclusion of their story in **Torn**. One-Click Torn now!*

Thank you for reading *Taken!* I hope you love Sebastian and Helena. Their story continues in *Torn*, the final installment in the *Dark Legacy Duet*.

Taking her is my right.
Breaking her, my duty.

I was always going to choose Helena. I knew it the instant I saw her.

She's different than the others. There's a darkness about her. Something wild inside her. And it calls to the beast inside me.

But she isn't what I expect. With every word and

every touch, she pushes me, burrows deep under my skin, challenging the rules, upending history.

And all the while, I see how my brother watches her. He wants her, and as the rules stand, she'll become his in one year's time.

Except that I have no intention of giving her up.

One-Click Torn Now!

If you'd like to sign up for my newsletter and keep up to date on new books, sales and events, click here! I don't ever share your information and promise not to clog up your inbox.

Like my FB Author Page to keep updated on news and giveaways!

I have a FB Fan Group where I share exclusive teasers, giveaways and just fun stuff. Probably TMI :) It's called The Knight Spot. I'd love for you to join us! Just click here!

ALSO BY NATASHA KNIGHT

Collateral Damage Duet

Collateral: an Arranged Marriage Mafia Romance
Damage: an Arranged Marriage Mafia Romance

Ties that Bind Duet

Mine

His

Dark Legacy Trilogy

Taken (Dark Legacy, Book 1)
Torn (Dark Legacy, Book 2)
Twisted (Dark Legacy, Book 3)

MacLeod Brothers

Devil's Bargain

Benedetti Mafia World

Salvatore: a Dark Mafia Romance
Dominic: a Dark Mafia Romance

Sergio: a Dark Mafia Romance

The Benedetti Brothers Box Set (Contains Salvatore, Dominic and Sergio)

Killian: a Dark Mafia Romance

Giovanni: a Dark Mafia Romance

The Amado Brothers

Dishonorable

Disgraced

Unhinged

Standalone Dark Romance

Descent

Deviant

Beautiful Liar

Retribution

Theirs To Take

Captive, Mine

Alpha

Given to the Savage

Taken by the Beast

Claimed by the Beast

Captive's Desire

Protective Custody

Amy's Strict Doctor

Taming Emma

Taming Megan

Taming Naia

Reclaiming Sophie

The Firefighter's Girl

Dangerous Defiance

Her Rogue Knight

Taught To Kneel

Tamed: the Roark Brothers Trilogy

ACKNOWLEDGMENTS

Cover Design by CoverLuv

Cover Photography By Eric David Battershell

Cover Model Zeke Samples

ABOUT THE AUTHOR

USA Today bestselling author of contemporary romance, Natasha Knight specializes in dark, tortured heroes. Happily-Ever-Afters are guaranteed, but she likes to put her characters through hell to get them there. She's evil like that.

Want more?
www.natasha-knight.com
natasha-knight@outlook.com

Printed in Great Britain
by Amazon